ZIA

By Scott O'Dell

ZIA

A Yearling Book

Published by
Bantam Doubleday Dell Books for Young Readers
a division of
Bantam Doubleday Dell Publishing Group, Inc.
1540 Broadway
New York, New York 10036

ISBN: 0-440-21956-6

Reprinted by arrangement with Houghton Mifflin Company
Printed in the United States of America

February 1995

10 9 8 7 6 5 4 3

Also by
SCOTT O'DELL

---

to Dorothy Markinko

ZIA

1

After one of the big storms that come in from the islands, our shore is covered with small clams. The clams are no larger than the end of your finger and the wind spread them out on the beach so thick it's hard to walk. The clams are blue and when you look either way, up or down the beach, all you can see for leagues are these tiny blue clams. That's why we call it the Blue Beach.

The great storms always come in the winter but this one came in June and the beach was covered with clams up to your ankles. Usually we raked them up, my brother and I, into baskets and took them back to the Mission. There we washed them and cooked them in a little fresh water. They made wonderful soup, these little blue clams, and we would make a whole meal out of a bowl of soup and a handful of tortillas.

On this morning, after the storm had raged all night, we went to the beach early to gather clams. But the storm had washed up so much that we forgot the clams for a while and went running along the beach searching for other things.

We had a plan and we never changed it. We called it *que busco primero, yo mantengo*. For instance, if Mando found something first that he wanted he would keep it, and if I found something first that I wanted I would do the same. But if Mando found a jar with syrup in it and I found a fishing line and a hook, then we would make a swap. If we saw something at the same time and we both shouted "mine," then we would draw sticks and the one who got the longer stick won. We had very strict rules, but sometimes we quarreled over things we both wanted. Then we wouldn't speak to each other for a day.

On this morning, as we waded through the clams and picked up many things—a clock, part of a sail, and a carpenter's plane—I saw something gray drifting at the edge of the surf.

"Mine," I shouted and ran toward it.

Mando ran too, shouting, "Mine! Mine!"

It was a boat, a boat that one of the big ships had lost and it had floated ashore.

We reached the boat at the same time. Mando was still shouting, "Mine! Mine!" He was so excited he just stood there looking at the boat and shouting.

I calmly walked over and put my hand on the bow.

"I saw it first. And it's mine. That's the rule, Mando."

There were tears in his eyes.

"But I will make you captain. I'll be the owner and you'll be the captain who steers it," I said.

This seemed to satisfy him. He rubbed his eyes and tried to smile.

There was a name on the stern of the boat. It was printed in English and all I could read was the first word, Boston. Then a "B" and then a blank space where the paint had peeled away and then the letter "Y." Two words.

The boat turned up at both ends and was six strides long and about two strides wide. There were three places to sit, places for four oars, but there was only one oar left, and a harpoon. It was a very stout boat and once it had been painted black.

"What can we do with it?" I asked Mando, who was still trying to master his disappointment. "What do you say, captain?"

Mando walked around the boat and picked up the oar and put it back. "We can't take it to the Mission. Someone would steal it the first night."

"If we put our name on it?" I asked. "And pulled it up the beach and turned it upside down?"

"Even if we took it into the chapel, they would steal it," Mando said.

He scratched his nose, which always helped him to think. I waited, having no thoughts of my own.

"I'll tell you what," he said at last, walking around the boat again, "We'll hide it."

"But where?"

"You know San Felipe lagoon? We'll hide it there."

"But how do we get the boat into the lagoon?" I said.

"We float it. We walk and push at the same time." He grabbed hold of the stern. "And we do it now. Now. In another hour everyone will be shouting and running around down here."

We floated the longboat with the first big wave and step by step, my brother pushing against the stern and me guiding it from the bow, we came to the mouth of San Felipe lagoon. The tide was beginning to ebb, but we steered into the lagoon. We had enough water under us to shove the boat ashore.

No one ever came here because, close by, at the far end of the lagoon, was a haunted cave. Bats flew out of it at dusk and at dawn they flew back.

Some said it was the home of a large snake. There were many bad tales about it. Everyone was afraid of the lagoon and the cave. Mando was, too, but he pretended that he wasn't.

Nevertheless, we covered the boat with brush and seaweed, just to be sure that no one would see it. Then we gathered our trophies along the beach, acting as though nothing had happened, and went back to the Mission, high above the beach on a hill.

2

THE SERVICE was just beginning and afterward I went to Father Vicente to confess that I had found a boat on the beach.

Father Vicente was young and had a bony face and eyes the color of chocolate. He was a kind man. I think he liked me and I liked him.

I sat down on the little bench and put my lips against the screen that separated us. I could not see him but I knew he was there, listening to me. Some of the fathers would act as if they were listening to you but you could tell that they were thinking of something else.

"This morning," I said, "I found a boat on the shore. It was washed up by the storm."

"What kind of a boat?" said Father Vicente from far off, as if he were talking from another world.

"It looks like the boats the whaling ships use

when they go out to kill whales. It had places for four oars but all were lost save one. And it had a harpoon and a long line fastened to the harpoon."

"Where is it now?"

"My brother and I hid it in San Felipe lagoon."

"Is there a name on the boat?" Father Vicente asked me.

"There is a word." I spelled it for him. "Then there's another word that begins with a 'B' and then there's a letter that is rubbed out and then another letter. 'Y.' "

"Boston is part of the name and the last word is Boy. *Boston Boy*," said Father Vicente. "She's a whaler from Boston and hunts beyond Santa Rosa Island and the crew visits us sometimes. I've not seen them for two years now. They used to come every year."

I waited and held my breath. Then I said, "I found the boat on the shore. Does it belong to the ship or does it belong to me? That is what I want to know."

"They may not come to look for it," Father Vicente replied.

"But if they do come and ask if we have seen their boat, what will you say?"

"I will say I have not seen it," said Father Vicente, "which is the truth, *verdad*."

"It is the truth," I answered, "but if they ask you if you have heard of the boat?"

"I will say, 'Yes, señores, I have heard that a whaleboat washed ashore in the storm. I have heard this, but I have not seen the boat.'"

"It is the truth, but does the boat really belong to them? It was theirs and it broke away and washed up on our beach. Can they say that it is still their boat whether it broke away and washed up or not? That is what I would like to know."

"By the law of the sea the whaleboat you found belongs to you."

"But maybe they will not come to look for it. They have many boats."

"The best. But, Zia, the boat is yours. That is the law. Furthermore, you possess it and possession is important in matters of this kind."

"I did not steal the boat," I said, still a little troubled in spite of Father Vicente's advice. "It was a gift from the sea."

Father Vicente was silent for a while. "What plans do you have for this boat?" he asked.

"Mando is the captain and we will go out and fish and dive for abalone," I answered.

"But together, Zia. Mando is not to go alone. Is that understood? Good. He is young and sometimes giddy in the head. If I had a boat I would not trust him. Not alone. Not outside the lagoon. Not even that far alone."

"Nor will I."

When I said good-bye to Father Vicente, I went

outside to the garden. Mando was waiting for me.

"Did you go to confession?" I asked him.

"Yes, to Father Merced."

"Did you tell him about the boat?"

"No. He does not care about boats. Nor does God," said Mando. "But we do not have a real boat yet. It has only one oar. You cannot go anywhere with one oar, except in circles. When we have a real boat, then I will tell somebody maybe. But not Father Merced."

He started off toward the beach. I called him back. "Listen, Mando. You are not to take the boat out of the lagoon except when I am with you. Understand?"

Mando nodded. "I am going now to find a branch. One that is straight. One that is straight and will make a good oar."

"Before you go," I said, "Promise me that you will not take the boat unless I am with you. Look me in the eyes and promise."

Mando looked at me, though it caused him an effort. He touched his lips with his thumb and made some gestures that had to do with god Mukat and with Zando, asking for their help.

"I promise," he said and went running off to look for a straight limb.

Where he found the limb I do not know but it was straight and strong and he spent hours on it in the Mission shop before and after his work in the fields. He used my boat's oar for a model and made his oar exactly like it in shape, though it was heavier than mine.

We took the oar to the lagoon early the next Sunday morning after the church service was over. It was a bright day. The tide was moving out and the sun sparkled.

"You take the light oar," Mando said, "the one on the right side."

I clambered into the boat and sat down beside him and we both began to row down the lagoon toward the sea. Just before you reach the end of the lagoon there is a small beach and here we went ashore. Mando had brought an adobe brick with him and he scraped the stern of the boat where the name was. He scraped it clean and from the sack he carried on his back he took a wooden sign about two feet long.

"I made it in the workshop. What do you think? A good joke, huh? I changed the name. Father Zurriga helped me and we made a new name. See."

He held it up. The plaque was painted in white letters. It said *Island Girl*.

Mando was pleased with his little joke. "*Boston Boy. Island Girl*. That's a better name, huh?"

"For Karana?"

"Named for you," Mando said. "For you, my

sister. Because all you talk of is going to the island."

He nailed the plaque to the stern of the boat and we set off again. At the end of the lagoon where it meets the sea there is a long spit of land, curved like a saber. The spit breaks the force of the waves and we had no trouble rowing to the end of it and into the open sea.

We did not go far, but rowed along the shore, just outside the line where the swells begin to gather and break. And as the sun grew hot we headed back for the lagoon.

3

ALL THE beachcombing we did for the next week was to find things for the boat—some rope, a cushion, a blanket, a box of fishhooks inside an empty wine barrel, a heavy piece of iron, two bottles the right size to fill with drinking water.

The next Sunday morning we did not leave the lagoon. We took the boat and turned it upside down and covered the bottom with tar we had heated in a pot. The tar had washed up on the beach in long strips. I do not know where it came from. Mando said it was sent by Mukat, but this I doubt. The boat had leaked a little before, but now that the bottom was covered with tar not a drop came in.

The following Sunday we picked up the heavy piece of iron where we had hidden it and fastened it to a chain I had found and fastened the chain to a rope. Now we had a boat that did not leak, that had two oars, and an anchor that was so heavy it took both of us to lift it.

"We should go somewhere now," Mando said. "Maybe around the world like Columbus."

"Columbus did not go around the world, Mando."

"Then we will be the first to go."

"Magellan went around the world first," I said, showing off the knowledge I had learned in the Mission school.

"Maybe we can go somewhere not as far," Mando said. "Maybe to the island."

"What island, Mando?" I knew the island he meant. The idea had been in my thoughts even at the moment I had first seen the boat. I thought about it all the time.

"To the Island of the Blue Dolphins," Mando said. "We will find Karana and bring her home." He paused and his face lighted up. "We could put a sail on the boat and sail sometimes when the wind was blowing. Then we could row when it was calm. We could do both. We could row and sail. In two days or three we would reach the island."

"Maybe she is not there now," I said.

"Maybe she is dead," said Mando. "Maybe wild dogs ate her up."

"It is possible," I said to put an end to these thoughts. "But the white man, Captain Nidever, saw her footsteps in the sand when he was there last year."

"Why did he not follow the footsteps? That's what I would like to know."

"There was a storm coming up and he feared for his boat."

"I will ask Mukat and Zando about these things. Then we will know. And maybe Father Merced also. No. Not him. Father Vicente? Maybe he will come with us. It would make it easier with three of us. Then I could fish while we sailed along. It would be easier even if I did not fish. But I am afraid of what Father Merced will say. Likewise Father Vicente. They may not allow us to go."

I felt angry. "We will go anyway, whatever is said. We are not chained to the earth. We have a boat and oars and an anchor. What are they for? They belong to us. To go out in San Felipe lagoon, is that what they are meant for?"

I had already made up my mind to make the voyage beyond the islands of Santa Cruz and Santa Rosa, out to the far island, where no one went, even the Chumash Indians in their red canoes. Nobody ever went there except the ship that came to rescue our tribe, except Captain Nidever, who was a hunter and went to the island to hunt otter. But we would go, my brother and I, now that we owned a seaworthy boat with two oars.

Yes, we would go and we would go soon. It was why I had come to Mission Santa Barbara in the first place. When Mando and I lived far to the south in the Cupeño village of Pala I had decided this.

That was the day two padres came to our village. They came on foot in their sandals and long robes and talked to our chief. They talked for a long time, all that day and into the night. There were more than a hundred of us and most of us listened.

One of the padres said, "Your people will be treated well. They will have plenty to eat. The work will not be heavy and they will have a good place to sleep, better than you have here." He paused to look around at our brush huts. "And we will teach you to speak Spanish and introduce you to our God, who will bless you and look over you."

"We have enough to eat," our chief said. "The huts you look at with scorn are not to our liking. Where we came from, where we lived before the Spanish and the white man drove us away from our meadows and springs, we had better places to live. And our gods, though they are different from yours, bless us with rain and sun and many places where we can go."

This was true.

Every year in the early summer we went to the sea and put up brush huts and fished. We ate some of the fish we caught and abalones we gathered on the rocks, but most of them we put on blankets in the sun and dried for winter.

We stayed on the beach, which was pretty and had white sand, and fished and dug for clams. We netted wild birds that came to a lagoon near where we camped and roasted them in a pit that we dug and covered with seaweed.

Until late summer we lived there on the beach. Then we gathered up our dried fish and our abalones and went back into our hills, which lay close against the mountains. There in the hills we women gathered acorns from the oak trees.

There was a great stone ledge and on this ledge we soaked the acorns and then let them dry in the sun. On the ledge were hundreds of holes that many women during their lifetimes had dug. In these holes, using stones, we ground the acorns to flour. We made many sacks of this flour.

With this flour and the abalone and fish we had gathered and the deer that our hunters ran down and killed, we lived through the winter. Our food sometimes ran low late in the spring. Then we dug roots and lived on those until it was summer and time to go to the sea again.

As we stood around our chief listening very

carefully, he said, "They have a home there in a place they call Santa Barbara. It is cool in summer and warm in winter. They have fields where they grow things like melons and the sea is not far off. They want us to come and live with them."

"What if we do not like this place?" the chief's son asked. "What if the sun does not shine like they say? And the sea is far away and has no fish in it?"

"We will come home then," the chief explained. "If it does not suit us we will take the trail and return."

One of the padres said, hoping to persuade us to leave, "The time has come for us to gather together, the Church and the Indians—both of us. And we must gather about the Missions, which, as you know, are many, a day apart on horseback from San Diego in the south to San Francisco in the north. They were meant to be forts, if need be, and so they are."

The other padre said, "First, the Mexican government took thousands of acres of our Mission lands. Then a war came between Mexico and the gringos, which the gringos won. Then the gringos took your lands and much of what was left of the Mission lands."

"The time has come for us to join together against the gringos, and the greedy Mexicans, and Spaniards," the first padre said. "Otherwise, there will be nothing left, not one acre, for any of us. Nothing! The white men and the Spanish women they married will have it all. They and the rich Mexicans and Spaniards. You will have nothing. Even less than you have now."

After that the two men talked for another day and on the third day seven of us went with them. We took everything we owned, some even took their dogs, though the padres said that it would be better if we left them behind in our village.

Mando went because he liked the sea and fishing. My friends Rosa and Anita went because they thought it all sounded adventurous and they would meet many boys. Everyone had a different reason for going, different from mine.

Mission Santa Barbara, where the padres were taking us, was near the Island of the Blue Dolphins. People, after my mother died, told me about my aunt who lived on this island and that she had lived there for many years alone. That was when I thought of going to Santa Barbara. I knew that there were Indians close by the Mission who owned canoes. Perhaps if I went there I could find one who would help me reach the island and bring Karana back. It was a wild thought, but it was why I left my home in Pala and followed the padres to the Mission at Santa Barbara.

I had never known my aunt, Karana. I was very young when my mother talked about the sister

18

she loved, so I have forgotten most of the things she said.

But from what people said I did remember that Karana had leaped from the ship that had come to rescue our small tribe from the Island of the Blue Dolphins and take it to the mainland where it would be safe from the Aleuts who sailed down from far in the north and killed our people. She had leaped from the ship because in all the excitement of leaving, their brother had been left behind and she swam back to search for him.

But the captain of the ship would not wait. He was afraid of a storm that was coming and would not stay until Karana found him. It was in this way that she had been left behind on the Island of the Blue Dolphins.

And yet I wondered sometimes if Karana would want to live here at the Mission, although it seemed to me that she must have yearned for the place where her people had gone. I wondered because some days I liked living at the Mission and there were days when I longed for our village in the mountains, far from the sea and the men who went around quietly in their sandals and Enrica who told us what we could do and not do.

But because of what I had been told I had grown up with my mind set upon finding Karana. It was a silent promise I had made to myself. This was why I went to the Mission Santa Barbara with

Father Vicente and why I stayed there when I was homesick for the mountains. It was the only way I could ever hope to find Karana, who was the last of my kin, except for Mando.

I remembered Captain Nidever who had made a voyage to the Island of the Blue Dolphins and had seen Karana's footsteps in the sand and had seen her fleeing up the cliff. Perhaps he would tell me about his voyage and give me advice that I could use.

4

T HE NEXT day I took Father Vicente's burro and went to see Captain Nidever. He lived in an adobe shack on a cliff not far to the south. From his house there was a steep trail down to the shore.

On this morning I found him there sitting in the sun. He was carving a ship out of a small piece of wood. He was making the ship inside a bottle, putting the pieces together with glue. I had never seen a ship with masts and sails on the inside of a bottle in my life before.

I waited until he paused and looked out at the sea. Then I asked him about my aunt, Karana.

"I never talked to her," he said, holding the bottle up to the sun and turning it first one way, then another. "She ran like a catamount over the rocks, up the cliff, and disappeared."

"But you saw her with your own eyes?"

"Saw her and her footsteps, too."

"It could not be a man that you saw?"

"Men don't look like women even on that island. No, I saw her and her footsteps. Plain as day."

I then asked him what I had come to ask. "How did you go, señor, when you went to the island? Did you go to the south of Santa Rosa or to the north?"

"To neither side. As you know there are two islands there, Santa Cruz on your left and Santa Rosa on your right. There is a channel, a narrow channel, between them. It is through this channel that you go."

He put the bottle on the blanket spread out before him and gave me a quizzical look. "You don't have any real idea in your head about sailing to Dolphin Island, do you?"

"Yes."

"In what?"

"A whaleboat. It floated ashore in the storm."

"How long is she?"

"About six strides long."

"About eighteen feet, then. They're seaworthy and tough, these whaleboats. Who's going with you?"

"My brother."

"How old is he?"

"Twelve." I stretched the truth only a little.

Captain Nidever picked up the bottle and said nothing for a long time.

"You and your brother," he said, "in an eighteen-footer. You've got more nerve than I have. There's a lot of water out yonder and heavy winds and rocks and reefs. What kind of a sail do you carry?"

"None."

"How do you get there?"

"We will row."

Captain Nidever snorted. "You know how far it is to Dolphin Island?"

I shook my head.

"Sixty miles if it's a foot. Have you ever rowed sixty miles through waves that sweep down from Alaska and a wind that seldom blows less than twenty-five knots?"

"No."

"Have you ever rowed six miles?"

"No."

Captain Nidever dabbed some glue on a splinter of wood and put it in the bottle using tweezers, holding his breath while he did so. Then he put the bottle down again and gave me a careful look.

"You're a strong girl," he said, "and your brother is strong too. But my advice is to stay home. You'll never make the island, what with heavy seas, fog and wind, no sails, and no experience."

I listened and was silent, but what Captain Nidever said did not change my mind. I got up and shook the sand from my skirt and thanked him for his advice.

"I'll be going out there one of these days," he said. "Got a deal with the Chumash, who live down the beach, for a couple of their big canoes. If it goes through I'll be leaving for the island sometime before summer's end. And this time I'll find your aunt. She's a regular mountain goat, the way she climbs cliffs. She has a dog as big as two dogs and she runs like a deer but I'll find her."

When I got back to the Mission and finished my daily work I went in search of my brother. He was in the shop, filing on a piece of iron that he was making into a fishhook.

"You have a hundred hooks already," I said.

"Now it is a hundred and one. This," he said, holding it up, "will catch the biggest *pez espada* that ever swam in the sea." It was thicker than his thumb and three times as long. "It will catch a whale."

"We are not going out to catch whales," I said, "or *espadas* either."

From that day on I began to save dried beef and food we could use for a week's voyage.

Mando said that we would live on what the sea brought us. Fish and lobsters, abalone and mussels from the rocks on the islands we passed.

"We will live off the sea with what I catch," he bragged. "You don't need to worry. I'll catch a duck or two also."

But I still saved food that would keep for a week or more, in case we failed to catch anything with all of Mando's hooks. The boat was well stocked by the time we were ready to go. Our store would last a week should we need it.

We told no one, not even Father Vicente. Nor Father Merced, who might tell Captain Cordova at the garrison, which was near the Mission, and have the captain put us in prison for stealing something that belongs to the Mission.

We planned to leave two nights before the full moon, after the last bell before bed. The afternoon before we left, Captain Nidever came to the Mission and told me again that it was a foolish thing to do.

"If you were a sailor. If you had experience on the sea, even on the water near our islands, I would say nothing. But you are going into a treacherous world of winds and seas that can be very rough in a very small boat."

Mando spoke up. "Mukat and Zando will guard us."

Captain Nidever looked puzzled, not having heard the names of our Indian gods before. He saw that we could not be persuaded, that we had stubbornly closed our minds.

"When you get to Santa Cruz, anchor on the far side of the island, close to shore, in the kelp bed."

"We have an anchor that weighs forty pounds," Mando said.

"When you drop her," he said, "climb to the highest ridge and look far off to your left. If the day is clear, you'll see the Island of the Blue Dolphins. Then with your compass, mark the direction."

"We have none."

"No compass? You'll end up in China."

He reached in his jacket and took out something that looked like a watch.

"Here's one I'm not using," he said. Captain Nidever showed me the marks and letters on its face. "The needle always points north, no matter how you hold it," he explained.

He turned the compass in his hand and I saw that the needle always pointed toward the chapel door, as if Mukat were holding it fast.

"Put the compass on a rock," he said, "and turn it until the needle points to the letter "N." Then you must sight off to the island and put down the direction you read exactly—the direction to the Island of the Blue Dolphins. When you leave, head the boat that way, but make sure the needle is always over the letter "N." Without currents and winds you shouldn't be off more than three miles by nightfall and maybe five miles by the next. But from that distance you'll easily see the island." He closed the lid of the compass and gave it to me. "Don't forget to bring it back," he said, moving off down the beach.

"I will bring it back," I promised him. "And Karana, too."

He stopped. "If it gets too rough and you're taking on water, don't be afraid to turn back. You can always try again, you know. Remember that he who turns his stern to wind and spray, lives to sail another day."

5

MANDO FOUND a piece of cloth for a square sail and made a small mast, but on the night we left, with the moon shining on the water and the sea calm, the sail blew away before we had gone a league.

We rowed all night, rowing together and one at a time, resting when our hands began to hurt. We followed the line of the surf that showed white in the moon. At dawn we were down the coast, near Mission Ventura.

The surf was heavy here. Off in the west I could see the cliffs of Santa Cruz and Santa Rosa. Mando caught a *dorado* near the surf but he was too tired to clean it, so we ate a strip of jerky and two tortillas apiece.

There was no wind, only swells coming from the northwest. Rowing was easy in the smooth water and we reached the kelp bed on the south point of Santa Cruz. We worked our way through the kelp into a quiet cove. We moored our boat with strands of kelp instead of the heavy anchor and waded ashore, carrying the fish Mando had caught.

We climbed the cliff, while it was still light. Off to the southwest I could see the outline of the Island of the Blue Dolphins. It looked near to us and clear, but I noticed that the water was not so calm between Santa Cruz and the Island of the Blue Dolphins as it was along the shore we had traveled during the night. On the horizon there were humps that looked like hills, but were really big waves.

I put the compass on a rock and turned it until the needle pointed to "N," as Captain Nidever had told me to do, and read the direction where the island lay.

We went back down the cliffs and built a fire of sticks and brush. We ate the fish and boiled mussels we pried off the rocks in the pot I had. We had a good meal, but the blankets I had brought were not heavy enough to keep us warm. It was cold and my hands hurt. I was glad to see the sun come up far across the channel.

It took Mando an hour, or so it seemed, to get his fishing line together. He tied the big hook he had made in the workshop to a piece of thin chain, and the chain to the lines and ropes he had

gathered during the past month and strung together and coiled in a wine barrel. None of the
lines were the same size or length, but they were
all very heavy.

"I'll catch a *pez espada* as big as the boat," he
said as we made our way out of the kelp and
started off toward the island. I kept the compass
in my lap while we rowed and looked at it from
time to time to make sure we were going in the
right direction, for we could no longer see the Island of the Blue Dolphins.

The wind was light and the waves had not built
up yet. Dolphins came and played around the
boat, back and forth across our bow. We saw five
whales moving south, blowing fountains of mist
in the air. Two flying fish came crashing aboard
and Mando fastened one on his big hook and let
out some of his line from the barrel.

"I'll catch an *espada* as big as the boat," Mando
said.

"What will you do with one that big?"

"Tow it home and haul it up on the beach for
everyone to see."

"You forget that we are headed for the island,
not for home," I reminded him. "Nor to catch
espadas."

It was clear to me that he thought of our voyage
as a chance to fish and of little else.

He picked up the whaling harpoon, which he had brought along, and stopped rowing to brandish it over his head like a sword.

Far out, behind us, as he was brandishing the harpoon, I saw a fin. It was large and shining and caught the morning sun. It was moving slowly toward us, smoothly, like a knife cutting through the water. Then it slowly sank and I thought of it no more.

Mando put his harpoon down in a handy place, should he need it.

The sun was warm and a light wind came up, which felt good. My hands hurt and I tried different ways of holding the oar. Mando did the same and we went along very slowly for a while. But I watched the compass and kept it pointing right, as Captain Nidever had explained to me.

Mando had a bare foot on the line where it ran out from the barrel. The line began to move and he took his foot away and grabbed hold of it.

"I think," he said and stopped suddenly. The line was moving in his hand. "I think I have something. Maybe Señor Espada."

"I saw a fin a while ago," I said.

"Where?"

"Behind us."

"Why did you not say you saw a fin?"

"Because it disappeared before I could speak."

"That is no reason."

"We are not here to fish for *espadas*. That is a reason."

As I spoke, Mando pitched forward, holding tightly to the line.

"Let go!" I shouted.

The line was ripped from his grasp or else he would have been yanked overboard.

"*Espada!*" he gasped.

The barrel that held the coiled line began to jump. Then it turned over. I reached out and wrapped my arms around it. Mando wrapped his arms around me. The line made a hissing noise as it came out of the barrel.

"How much is left?" Mando said.

My face was close to the barrel and I could see the coils of line clearly. "Less than half."

The boat, as we stopped rowing, began to rock. It turned its beam to the waves that had come up and that made it rock worse.

"I'll hold the barrel," I said to Mando. "Take the oars and turn the bow into the wind."

He unloosened his hold on me and took up the oars. The boat righted itself.

The line was singing now. There was less than a third of it left.

"Brace yourself," I shouted to Mando.

At the same time I wedged the barrel under the

forward thwart and held it there, with my feet braced against an oak rib.

Before we left Mando had bored a hole in the bottom of the barrel, passed the line through the hole and tied a double knot. There was no way the line could come free.

The last loop whirred past my ear. There was a jar and the whole boat shivered, as if we had struck a rock. The line was taut as iron but it did not break. I clung to the barrel that was wedged against the thwart, using all my strength. Mando kept our bow into the wind. The pull on the line grew steady and now we were moving slowly toward the island.

"Maybe he will tow us to where we want to go," Mando said. "I'll speak to Zando and he will speak to Señor Espada."

He said something under his breath and made a sign with three fingers. The great fish moved toward the island in a straight line. He was swimming deep but straight for the Island of the Blue Dolphins.

To ease the strain I asked Mando to throw a double rope around the barrel and tie it down. Then I let go of the barrel and took hold of the line. It was as thick through as my little finger and big and rough.

The wind shifted and the waves grew stronger.

We started to take water aboard. We bailed as best we could and kept the water ankle deep.

The sun was overhead. It was hot and bounced off the sea. We were moving slower than we could row, but we moved. Then the line slanted at a different angle. It moved straight down and swung the boat around. We were now headed in the direction of Santa Cruz, which we had left at dawn.

After a time the line slackened. I pulled on it, putting a dozen coils and more back in the barrel again. Then a dozen more.

"We have lost him," said Mando.

"No, he is coming up. He is coming toward the boat."

The fish came on. The barrel was half full of line now. But there must have been three hundred feet out.

"Does he come still?" Mando asked.

"Still, but not fast."

"It is big," he said.

"Maybe a marlin?"

"Too early for the señor. I have never seen him here in June. Nor has anyone. He comes from the south only when the sea is warm."

"How big do you think he is?"

We had now been hooked up to him since soon after dawn and now the sun was on its way into the west.

"He must be immense, Zia."

"How immense?"

"As big as three big men. If he was not, he would not pull us all over the ocean."

Mando knew more about the *pez espadas* than any fisherman at the Mission. He could tell them just by their fins when they lay far off sunning themselves.

The heavy line quit coming. I braced my feet against the ribs of the boat and pulled. We pulled together. But the fish slowly took the line out of our hands and then out of the barrel again.

"There is no more line left and he now pulls us," I said. "There has been a strain on the barrel all day. It might collapse sometime."

"I selected a barrel I have used before and have faith in," Mando said. "It is made of oak that is an inch in thickness. And it has five iron bands around it. It will hold as long as the line holds and that will be a long time. Make yourself comfortable and have patience. He will tire before we do."

I was tired already. My hands were bleeding.

"Place them in the water," Mando said. "But one at a time. I have a heavy load up here." He was braced at the bow, with the line looped once around the bit. "The salt water makes them feel better. Worse for a while, then better."

"I do not feel them at all," I said. "They are

numb. They are not mine. They belong to someone else."

"Not to me. I already have a pair that are
numb."

We rounded the kelp bed at the south point of
Santa Cruz, moving slowly. It was better now.
The sun was on my back and not in my eyes, and
the water was not so rough. But I was tired and
very angry.

"Remember again we did not come to fish for
espadas," I said. "I am going to cut the line. Then
we will turn around and go ashore and in the
morning start for the island once more."

"You will cut the line with what?" Mando
asked. "I have the knife. I have it in my belt.
Perhaps you can cut the line with your teeth.
They are big like the fish's teeth and you have
many of them."

The drag stopped and the line no longer
slanted out.

"He is going down. That is a good sign," said
Mando.

He unloosened the line looped on the bit and
we both took it in hand over hand.

"He is under us now," Mando said. "And coming up. Slow. But he comes."

We peered over the side of the boat and
watched for him in the water that was clear but a
deep blue.

6

NIGHTFALL had come on gently. There was no
wind and the sky was clear except for pink streaks
in the west where the sun had been. I was trailing
one hand in the cool water. Then I shifted across
the thwart and trailed my other hand. They were
still numb but they did not hurt so much and the
blood had stopped.

Mando's cry must have been heard by those at
the Mission, even by those who were asleep. I
heard the cry before I saw the fish.

"*Grande!*" shouted Mando. "*Un gran pez
espada.*"

When I saw it first it was in the air about fifty
yards off to our right. It seemed to be standing on
its scythelike tail. The hook that Mando had made
and polished in the workshop had gone into the
bone of the fish's underjaw. His sword was longer

than my arm and he thrashed it from side to side in an attempt to throw off the hook.

With a great splash he fell back in the water, into the same hole he had come from.

"Hold tight," Mando shouted. "But not too tight. Give him a chance to run."

The fish took out some line and jumped again and thrashed his sword. But he did not come in. He took out more line and we tied it to the bit and gave him the boat again to carry.

It was too dark to see now. By the evening star and then by the position of the Big Bear, the only constellation I knew, I thought we must be moving north and toward the coast. But I was not sure, though the compass pointed in the right direction. Even in the channel the night wind was sharp and full of spray.

"Do we have tortillas?" Mando asked.

"Four apiece," I said and handed them up to him.

"And water."

I gave him the jug, which was half empty. "Do not drink like a camel," I cautioned him.

"How does a camel drink?" he asked.

Mando felt very good. He was thinking of all the praise he would receive when he got back to the Mission.

"The camel drinks all the water he can hold," I said. "And then he goes without water for weeks.

Sometimes he bursts himself wide open after he drinks so much at one time."

"The fish will not last for weeks," Mando said. "He will last through the night. He will go slow now and wait for daylight. Then he will thrash about and put on a big fiesta and it will be his last."

Mando ate the four tortillas, taking his time, and drank one long swig of water. Then he sat for a while. Then he talked and by the time the moon was overhead he was asleep, snoring. He was without a worry.

I was too tired to sleep and afraid that we would run ashore, either on Santa Cruz Island or the coast. I was not sure where we were. We seemed to be following along the kelp bed that rimmed the island, but I could be wrong. The sea is not a good place to be when you are tired and hungry and worried. At no time is it a place to do foolish things.

At the first false dawn, a pearly gray in the east, I was aware that we were no longer moving. We were, as I had thought, near the kelp beds. The line was slack as if it had been broken. At some time during the night I could have fallen asleep and the fish could have broken free.

I began to take in the line, cautiously at first, and then hand over hand. As it came in I coiled it carefully in the big barrel. Mando lay in the bow, one hand trailing in the water, asleep as if he had never slept before.

The sun was up by the time that I caught sight of the big fish. He was about five boat lengths away and scarcely moving. Only his tail moved and very slowly. The way the rising sun slanted he was in the shadow of the boat, but I could see that he was about three arm's lengths away. My hands still bled and I guided the fish up to us, not forcing him. I crouched in the bottom of the boat, keeping out of sight, and making as few movements as possible.

I had the line wrapped around my left wrist as I brought him up, a foot at a time, putting my knees on the line as each strip came in. The sun was in Mando's face, but he did not move. He had a wonderful look as if he were listening to some heavenly music. All I could hear was the surf beating against the shore and then the sounds of the waves washing back from the cliffs and caves.

The big fish was not a *pez espada*, as Mando had thought it to be. His bill was a round spear, very long, and curved upward a little. His back was a purple blue and light blue bands ran from his back to his undersides, which were silver. I had seen marlin before and this was a marlin, a big one, the size of three large men and almost as long as the boat.

The fish stopped and I held the line softly, not

moving, trying not to breathe. The hook was there in his lower jaw and looked solid. He came forward so that his pointed bill was even with the bow of the boat. His tail was barely moving. The big fin on his back caught the sun and showed violet and blue spots.

I crouched, watching him. His eyes moved, looking up at the boat and then at me. They were immense and once they had found me they did not shift away. In the sun they looked golden, but they were of different colors, some of the colors that were on his back.

His gaze did not move from me. It was strange to look into the eyes of a fish that looked back at you. It seemed to me, as I crouched there, that in his mind he knew that I was the cause of the hook in his mouth and the long fight through the day and the dark. And yet I saw no hatred in them. Only a sort of wonderment and surprise and besides all a look of submission.

Mando was sleeping, fighting off a cloud of gnats, but still in his sleep. I was close enough to him to touch his outstretched foot with mine. I thought of waking him, but feared that he would jump and arouse the fish into a last effort to free itself.

The harpoon and a gaff made of a long bamboo rod and iron lay within my reach. I could use either one. Or if I thought and planned carefully

41

I would be able to use both on the great fish.

He was now even with the boat, leaning against it as if to rest. I could not see the marlin's eyes any longer. Only his purple back and the blue bands running down his sides. But I remembered his eyes and their look of surprise and submission. I could think of nothing else but his eyes looking at me.

Mando was asleep on his side. Leaning forward, I slipped his long knife from its sheath. I unloosed the line from my wrist and set it down squarely on the gunwale. The knife was sharp and it went through the line quickly.

The big fish had not moved. He did not know yet that he was free. I stood up and as I did the boat rocked against him. He started to move away. I tossed the severed line over the side. The fish saw the movement and began to edge away from the boat. He slanted downward, his fins barely moving. He became a long shadow and then a small shadow and was gone.

The iron hook in his jaw and the line would be eaten away in time by the sea, which ate everything. I sat back and for a while watched Mando sleeping. Then I picked up the oars and began to row.

The morning was clear and there was no wind. I headed back, up the coast toward the Mission of Santa Barbara. In one part of me I was glad the marlin had come between us and the ocean.

Mando was still asleep when we rounded Santa Cruz. It was midmorning. I gave him a kick in the shins and he came awake, staring about as if he had no idea where he was, on land or on the sea. But in one glance he saw that the big fish had gone.

He jumped to his feet. "What happened? *Qué pasa?* My *pez espada*. Where is he?"

The line I had cut lay at his feet beside his knife. Mando glanced at the line, at his knife, then at me.

"He is gone," I said. "He left while you were asleep."

Mando picked up the line I had cut and looked at it. "The line did not fray. It did not break from the fish's strength. The line was cut." He picked up his blade. "It was cut with a sharp knife. Like this one. I did not know that the *pez espada* carries a knife."

"They do not carry knives. Only people carry knives," I said. "When did we hook the fish?"

"Yesterday, in the morning."

"Then he was with us for almost a day," I said. "How would you like to be with a boat for almost a day at the end of a line—with an iron hook in your mouth? Would you like that, Señor fisherman? How would you like half a day? Or perhaps an hour would suit you better."

43

"I am not a fish."

"If you were, amigo, would you like an iron hook in your mouth?"

"You talk foolish talk," Mando said. "People are not fish."

"But fish also bleed. How would you like the blood for an afternoon and a night and a morning. How would the *sangre* taste, brother Mando?"

"No tiene nada en la cabeza," Mando said, put his knife back in its sheath, and stretched out to sleep again. "Next time I fish among fishermen," he said with great disgust.

"I have enough in my head," I answered, "to know that you are a poor sailor and when I go anywhere again it will be alone."

"I am still here," he said, looking at me through half-closed eyes. "I am still a sailor."

"About to fall asleep."

"I am still here," I repeat. "We have lost more than a day, but the weather is good. We have enough food. Let us continue what we have begun."

I nodded my head, yet I was afraid of the wind and the wild seas I had seen. I was afraid all over—in my stomach and in my head.

7

We were now near the southern tip of Santa Cruz Island, not far from where we had started. Night was coming and I thought it best to wait and leave early in the morning before the wind came.

There was a small headland near us. I had noticed yesterday afternoon that there was a good anchorage beyond it. It was in a cove protected from waves and wind.

"Take an oar," I said to Mando. "*Vámanos!*"

"I thought I was the captain," he replied.

I shoved an oar into his hand and we began to row toward the cove. As we rounded the promontory, I saw close off our bow a large whaling ship. On each side of the ship floated a dead whale. Fires were going on deck and a cloud of oily smoke drifted toward us.

The smoke was so thick it was hard to see, but gradually I made out on the ship's stern, printed in gold letters, the name *Boston Boy*. We were now within shouting distance of the ship.

Quietly I said to Mando, "The ship is the one that lost its longboat in the storm. Do as I say and do not talk. Push with your oar while I pull with mine and we will circle back and go the way we came. Use your oar deliberately and slowly, while I do the same. If God is with us they will not see that the boat we are rowing is the boat they lost."

"I will speak a word to Mukat," my brother whispered, and began to mumble to himself.

"Push on your oar and be quiet. Nor look in their direction."

"Our boat has a new color and a new name," Mando said. "They will not recognize it."

"If they do we are in trouble," I answered. "Now that we have made our turn, I will row and you put out your fishing lines. They will think we are fishermen, maybe."

The smoke from the fires grew thin but we were less than half a league from the promontory. Once beyond it we could not be seen from the ship. I began to row faster, until I thought my lungs would burst. The boat was heavy and not meant for two oarsmen.

We reached the headland and pulled into the

cove, out of sight of the ship. We had outwitted the Anglos. We were safe.

"Mukat heard me," Mando said.

As he spoke these words, a longboat rounded the headland. It was the same kind of boat as ours. Four men were at the oars and one sat in the bow. They rowed to where we were drifting. They rowed around us once in silence. They were black from the fire and whale smoke. Then they all shipped their oars except one who kept his oar in the water and steered.

One of the men had blue eyes. He stood up and spoke to me.

"Where did you get the boat?" he asked.

"At the Mission Santa Barbara," I said.

"How long have you had it? Since the storm?"

"Yes," I said, "since the storm."

"It washed ashore?"

"Yes."

Mando spoke up. "I painted it and worked on it and gave it a new name," he said.

"So I see," the man with the blue eyes said. "But the boat is ours. It is one we lost in the storm. We lost two men also."

"The boat belongs to us," I said. "Father Vicente says that there is a law. Because it washed ashore and we found it, it is ours."

"That is the law," Mando said. "Father Vicente vows it."

A man who sat in the bow of the longboat and had said nothing spoke up now. He had a face with many wrinkles, though he was a young man, and the tip of one of his ears was missing. In the other he wore a heavy gold earring with a pearl in it.

"Enough talk," he said. He had a deep voice and he bit the ends of his words off. "We have work to do. Put them ashore and be done with them."

"We can use another hand," the man with the blue eyes said. "John Tucker turned up sick this morning and last night Woods got his arm burned bad. The young one looks like he could do a little stoking. And the girl can help in the galley. Cook us up some of those Mexican tortillas and frijoles."

"Makes sense to me," one of the whalers said. "We'll get in trouble with the Mission if we leave them on the island."

The young man in the bow said nothing for a while. He was looking us over carefully. Then he said, "Women on the ship bring bad luck. Usually, that is. But once on the *Caleb Stone* the captain had his wife along and we killed seven whales in one day. Killed five the next. We almost sank with oil. We split a good thirty thousand on that voyage. The best of the season."

He gave a signal and one of the whalers jumped aboard with a rope in his hand. He tied it to our bow and went back and took up his oar. The four men began to row, towing us after them.

My brother and I sat silent and fearful.

The young man with the blue eyes called back to us, "Give us a hand. This is no free boat ride."

Mando and I took up our oars and began to row. I did not row hard. Nor did Mando, who kept his eyes on the rope that was towing us, as if he had a mind to cut it.

I spoke to him in Indian dialect, so the Anglo whalers would not understand.

"Do not use your knife. On the rope or on the white men. They are many and there are two of us. They will kill us and not think twice about it. Be polite and do as you are told."

"I will use my knife tonight while they sleep."

"You will do nothing with your knife nor with your tongue."

"I will speak to Mukat," Mando said.

"Speak to Mukat all you wish. But to the white men say nothing."

We rounded the headland and set off in the direction of the whaling ship. It was still billowing smoke. Through the smoke I could see fires burning and men moving about on the deck and on the carcasses of the two dead whales. It looked like the scene Father Vicente described to us sometimes—like the smoke and fires of Hell.

When we reached the ship the blue-eyed man

told us to climb a rope ladder that was dangling over the ship. "Step lively," he said, which we did, though the ladder swayed and the ship rolled. He came up after us and took me to a place in the bow where food was cooking on a brick stove. I was not there a second before the cook thrust a knife into my hand and pointed out a basket of potatoes. He said nothing but made motions, which meant that I was to peel them.

I did not know what happened to Mando until noon when the men came in to eat. He was as oily and black as the rest and when he spoke his teeth glistened white against his skin.

"What do you do?" I whispered to him.

"I toss hunks of blubber into the pots," he whispered back. "The heat and the smoke are bad. And the smell, it does something to the stomach. Tomorrow I will go crazy and jump overboard. Maybe I will go crazy before tomorrow."

8

THE COOK was fat and enjoyed eating. He enjoyed chewing tobacco, too, which he carried in a leather pouch. He enjoyed both so much that he chewed and ate at the same time, holding the tobacco under his lower lip while he munched away. He spat a lot, sometimes in the fire. But the next morning when I helped him slice up the beef the mate had bought on shore he told me to take my time and not get in a hurry.

"This is no boarding house where they have to eat on the stroke of the hour," he said. "Here we serve mess when it's ready. Not a minute before."

In the afternoon he gave me some time and urged me to look around the ship.

"The *Boston Boy* is not a very pretty sight right now," he said. "But you can hold your nose and look where you want. If the men give you any lip, give it back to them. But mostly they're gentlemen—the rough sort, mind you. Besides, they've got no time for chatter."

He walked to the door of the galley, which ran from one side of the ship to the other, spat to windward, and came back.

"We ran into some sperm whales," he said. "What they're doing around here—usually it's the grays—nobody knows. But we caught us two and since we're on shares everybody is killing himself to fill every barrel on shipboard."

I was not interested in watching the men slice off the blubber in great long strips with their sharp flensing knives and haul the whales aboard with big hooks and fling them into the trying pots. I wanted to talk to my brother Mando and see if together we could think of some way to get away from the ship.

Most of the ship—all of the middle part—was given up to boiling the blubber. In front of one of the brick furnaces I found Mando. He was stripped to the waist and was feeding the fire under the pots. He had a pair of tongs and would reach in the pot and pull out pieces that no longer had oil in them and then fling them into the fire, where they blazed up and added mightily to the heat.

He glanced at me but there was no chance to talk. I tried to meet him that night after supper but I could not find him. It was not until the third day, in the afternoon, that an accident happened to the mate, the young man with the wrinkles and the gold earring, that gave us a chance to talk.

The mate had talked a lot at noon when he was eating, bragging about how rich everyone was going to be, now that a girl was aboard.

"Nothing but luck," he had said, "from now until the time we sight Boston port. Fair seas at the Cape, following winds, good weather."

He was talking to all the sailors who thought that it was bad luck to have a woman on the ship. There were many of them and I hoped they would cause a mutiny and put me ashore, but the very next day, the ship killed four more sperm whales, who the young mate said were a thousand miles from their usual haunts.

"Proves I was right," he bragged, and furthermore we'll take an Indian to Boston and show the citizens of that proper town what real Indians look like. No feathered savages, these ones."

He gave me an admiring smile. The smile and what he had said about taking us away and showing us off to strange people made me more determined than I ever was to flee from the ship.

He drank down the last of a flagon of wine he had bought nearby at Mission Ventura and went reeling on deck. I had cleaned up the table and was getting ready to wash the dishes with the help of a dwarf South Sea Islander they had picked up somewhere—and were also going to take to Boston—when I heard a scream, then the running of feet and the shouts of many men.

The commotion was caused by a strange accident that had befallen the earringed mate, whether from the wine he had drunk at the noon meal or from an odd misfortune, I do not know.

I had never seen a sperm whale before. The whales that live on our coast are different. They have a more fishlike look about them for one thing. But the sperm whale has a prow for a nose, like a great rock that rises straight from the sea. It forms a fourth part of the animal. The cook had told me this the first day when he had set me to peeling the basket of potatoes.

When Mando and I had first set foot on the ship, I had noticed an enormous head hanging at the bulwarks, held there by iron hooks fastened to ropes strung from above.

While I was peeling the basket of potatoes the cook had set before me, I asked him about this enormous head, which had loomed beside me when I had climbed on deck. I remembered the fright I had felt at this great dangling maw with its ivory teeth that looked as long as my arm. Beyond it hung still another of these giant heads, its mouth gaping open.

"Pure ivory," said the cook. "Valuable, but it's the head that's the treasure. Full of spermaceti, it is. Enough to fill five casks. It makes the finest perfume, young lady, this sweet-smelling whale oil."

"I have none," I said.

"If you did, here's where it would come from."

I ran out of the galley at the sound of screams and running feet. The cook followed me. Men were clustered around one of these hanging whale heads, some with knives, others with spades. They were all talking at once.

Mando grabbed my arm. "It's the mate. The one with the gold earring," he said. "He has fallen and will drown."

The mate, it seemed, had insisted upon cutting into the heads. This was his task, one that no one else could do so well. Not only to cut into the animal at the proper place but to manage the bailing out of the precious liquid it held in its enormous head.

After the iron bucket had gone down more than a dozen times, like a bucket into a well, and come back filled, the mate somehow had slipped and fallen deep down into the whale's skull, which was like a deep cavern.

His screams came up from the cavern, growing louder and louder while the men stood by, planning how best to reach him. First the iron bucket was taken from the pole and the pole lowered into the well. But, for some reason, the mate did not grasp it.

His screams grew fainter. Then someone with a flensing knife hacked at the underside of the whale's skull. The precious liquid poured out and with it the mate. He fell into the sea, drifted face downward, and before anyone could reach him sank from view. A few oily bubbles marked the place where he had gone down. Then the hat he had worn bobbed up and the sea was quiet.

All the ship's longboats, including ours, were manned. They went around in circles over the place where the mate had disappeared, but all they found was the hat he had worn, glistening with the precious oil that covered the sea.

9

It was the drowning of the mate that gave us a chance to escape from the *Boston Boy*.

The crew spent the rest of the afternoon searching for his body. They rowed in ever widening circles around the ship, using all of the longboats, of which they had five, including ours.

They searched until dusk when hunger drove them back to the ship. I was in the galley with the cook, the only sailor aboard who did not man an oar, except my brother and the captain, who kept mostly to his cabin, which was astern of us. From time to time during the afternoon he would appear on deck, hoist a spyglass to his eye, search the movement of each boat and then disappear.

Between peeling potatoes and cutting up strips of salt pork I had an opportunity to speak to

Mando. After the third day the captain had decided to make him a cabin boy. I guess he had seen him tending fire under the trying pots and was taken by the way he did his work.

In any event the captain had him dressed up in a white sweater and white pants—the only pants that Mando had ever owned—and kept him busy running errands. One of the errands that afternoon brought Mando to the galley for a cup and a crock of tea.

After the cook had made the tea and given it to my brother I followed him to the deck. He hurried along, me at his side, but we had a brief chance to speak.

"I heard the captain talking," said Mando. "He was talking to the second mate who is the first mate now. He said that the casks were full of oil and that they would sail for home tomorrow and for him to get everything ready."

"Then this is the last night we will have a chance to flee," I said.

"The captain also told the new mate that he was taking us with him to Boston. Wherever that is."

"I think it is far away," I said. "But wherever it is I am not going. I will jump overboard first and swim to the island."

"It is a long swim," Mando said. "And what would we do on the island?"

"We could find enough food to eat. We would wait until someone at the Mission found us. We could make fires and signal them," I said.

"There are many sharks out there, Zia. They were gnawing hunks out of dead whales all day. One of the men shot three, but more, many more, came back to eat."

There was a look in his eye and a tone to his words that surprised me and suddenly made me suspicious. "You are not thinking of going with the ship?"

"I have thought of it," Mando said.

"But you are not going?"

"I have no choice in these matters. Nor do you. We are the captives of the white men."

The idea of being a captive was something new for him. He seemed to like it.

"No," I said, "I am not a captive. Nor are you."

He began to move away. "I have to take the tea to the captain," he said.

"The captain can wait for his tea. Do you think we can find our boat in the dark?"

Mando stopped. "We can find it, but it will have no oars. They take all the oars on the ship at night."

"Because there are others who would like to escape also," I said. "That is why they hide the oars?"

Mando shrugged and started on his way. I followed him along the deck, within a few feet of the captain's door.

"Where do you sleep at night?" I said.

"In a locker over there." He pointed to a shelter nearby, without a door.

"Do you hear the ship's bell when it strikes?" I said.

"Sometimes I hear it. Sometimes not when I am sleeping."

"Tonight stay awake and hear it," I said, "when it strikes six times." I held my hands out and counted six on my fingers. "Six times means it is eleven o'clock."

"At the Mission six bells means six o'clock," said Mando. "Time to go and eat."

"Here they mean eleven o'clock. By then everyone will be asleep, except the man who watches the deck. Meet me here at the rail when you hear the six bells. And bring your knife."

"What if I do not choose to hear the bells," Mando said.

"You are eleven years old but you have not reached manhood," I said.

"I will be twelve in a moon or so," Mando said defiantly. "So I am twelve."

He lingered. "How can we run the boat without oars?" he asked. "We have no sail, either. How do we move?"

"We both can hold on to the rudder and kick our legs, as if we were swimming."

"What of the sharks?"

"There are more of them here on the ship than in the sea," I said. "Many more. And the captain is one of them."

"In the morning the captain will find that we are gone," Mando said. "He will send the boats out to search for us."

"We will be near Mission Ventura by morning. The current runs strong here in the channel and it runs toward the shore."

"I do not like what you say," Mando replied. "I do not like being without oars or a sail. What if the men who watch through the night see us? What of the sharks? What if the men search for us in the morning? What if they find us and put us in chains? There are two in chains now. They live in a dark hole down where the oil is stored." Mando walked toward the captain's door. "I do not like it," he said.

"We will find a way to reach Karana and bring her home to the Mission," I said. "She belongs to our tribe. She belongs to us especially. I left my home to find her."

Night was falling. The boats were coming back from their search. The men were tying them up and climbing the rope ladder.

"Do not forget," I said. "We are slaves to no

61

one. Nor are we something for people to stare at. Remain awake. Listen for the six bells. And come promptly with your knife."

I went back to the galley, to the storeroom where I slept. I put some of the beef left from supper in a bag with a handful of big round crackers, hard as stones. From the rack beside the stove I took the sharpest knife the cook owned and put it into the bag. Then I sat down to wait for the six bells to strike.

Whether Mando would defy me and decide to remain with the ship and the white men, I did not know. But I knew that somehow I would find my way to shore.

10

At the sixth stroke of the ship's bell I took my bag, which held food, a knife, and a flask of water, and went to the galley door.

I had noticed as I sat waiting in the galley that the man on watch had walked the deck on the opposite side of the ship. He had walked to the bow and then to the stern. Then he stayed at each place for several minutes, then walked slowly back. He never walked on the left side of the ship because casks of whale oil were piled there.

One of his boots squeaked and I could hear each step that he took. He was now at the stern. I looked around the corner of the galley door and saw him standing there by the wheel gazing out at the sea. The ship's ladder hung from the bulwarks, not far from where he stood.

I waited in the shadows until I heard the

squeak of his boot pass the galley door. Quietly in my bare feet I slipped out and ran along the deck to the place near the captain's door where I was to meet Mando. He was not there. I could hear the squeak of the watchman's boot. He had reached the bow of the ship. He would stand there for a short time and then come back.

I decided that if Mando did not come at once I would go myself. There was a small moon and I could see the top of the ladder, the two iron hooks that held it to the bulwarks. I ran toward it, climbed over, and found the first step.

The sea was dark. The boats were tethered to a long boom at the bottom of the ladder. I heard a sound beneath me as I went down and as I came to the last rung I saw a figure crouching in one of the boats. It was Mando. I saw the dull flash of his knife. He was cutting the rope that held the first of the longboats. It was a boat that the captain used.

"Take ours," I whispered to him.

"It is the last one out," he answered.

Above me I heard the tread of the watchman moving back from the bow. I jumped into the boat where Mando was hacking at the rope. "Crouch and make no noise," I said.

The watchman passed us and went to the stern. He came back slowly and stopped at the head of the ladder. I held on to Mando and both of us did not move until the watchman went on. Then Mando began to hack at the rope again.

"There is a knot in the rope. Have you tried to untie it?" I asked.

"I have tried. It is a special knot and I can do nothing with it."

"Let us take our boat," I whispered.

"What does it matter?" Mando said.

"It is ours," I said and climbed out of the captain's boat and into the one alongside.

Mando followed me. "A boat is a boat," he said.

"*Island Girl* is smaller and easier to handle," I said to end the argument.

We had reached her when I heard the squeak as the watchman moved above us. We crouched until he passed and came back. Then we both hacked hard at the rope that held us to the boom and freed ourselves.

I let myself over the side and, kicking my feet, slowly moved the boat to the side of the ship where the watchman did not pass.

Above us hung the monstrous heads. We passed a carcass and a second carcass, which had been stripped of all its fat. Mando took hold of the bones and helped me move the boat. Halfway along I told him to shove us away.

We left the carcass, moving with the tide and the waves in the direction of the island. Mando was in the water beside me. If the watchman had passed along our side of the ship he could have seen us. Still, if he had looked toward the island when he stood at the bow or the stern, he could have seen us, too, even though we were moving slowly and quietly, grasping the rudder.

When the first light showed in the east, we reached the kelp bed that surrounds the island. The kelp was heavy and we could not push through it. We climbed in the boat and lay there, resting and trying to get warm. I looked off toward the coast. It was dim and far away.

"The tide is against us," I said. "We will rest and wait for a while. But we should go on. They will be out looking for us, and the first place they look will be here."

"It is another hour before breakfast," Mando said. "They will eat and go on deck. It will be two hours before anyone will notice that a boat is missing. Maybe it will be longer."

I wondered if, after all, he wanted to be caught and taken back to the ship.

"The cook will miss me in the galley," I said. "And the captain will miss you when his morning tea is not brought on the silver tray. They will know we are gone before the hour is out."

I looked again at the distant shore. It was too far away to see the sand dunes or the waves breaking. The island was between us and the ship and I could not see her either.

It was then that I noticed the rudder. It was made of three oar-shaped slats, each one longer than my arm, and fastened to the boat with light iron straps. I dug my knife into the wood and saw that we could free the bolts that held it.

By the time the sun was rising we had the rudder off. The three slats were held together by wooden pegs. We broke them loose and had two pieces that we could use as paddles.

"*Vámanos!*" I said. "The wind is with us and the tide soon will be."

Mando looked over his shoulder, in the direction of the ship. Slowly he put his paddle in the water and we set out for the distant shore.

When the sun was well up we had cleared the island and could see the three masts of the ship on the horizon. The makeshift paddles were not as good as oars, but we were gaining headway nonetheless. The tide and wind were with us and the mainland now was clear. I could see the tower of Mission Ventura.

Mando was torn between the shore and the ship. He kept looking back over his shoulder until the topmost masts disappeared. From time to time, even then he would look back and sigh.

"You are sorry," I said, "that they did not send out their longboats and catch us."

"Nothing happens at the Mission," he said. "You work in the fields and clean the weeds out of the water ditches and sweep up the courtyard and light the candles."

"On the *Boston Boy* you would carry tea to the captain. That is all," I replied. "It is not much. But if you want to be a sailor, Father Vicente will see that you find a place on one of the ships. Maybe a ship where you will be a sailor and not a servant."

I had never been on this Ventura shore before in a boat. It looked like the shore at Santa Barbara farther up the coast, but there was a spit of land that ran out that had a rocky point. Between the spit and the shore was a cave. The water seemed to be quiet there and the breakers smaller than they were farther to the south. It was this cave that I aimed for.

As we approached the breakers and were squaring the boat, holding it back as best we could to catch one of the smaller waves, a current caught us. It had foam around its edges and was running swift in a line with the beach toward the rocky spit.

"Paddle hard away from the shore," I shouted to my brother. "That way we may free ourselves from the current."

We both put all our strength into turning the boat away from the breakers, thinking that we could wait until the current let us free.

But the current, with its white edges, held the boat and bore us past the cave and toward the rocks, as if we were a chip of wood.

"Be ready to jump," I said.

We were both good swimmers and as the boat struck the rocks and keeled over we jumped. The water was cold. For a while we had to fight the tide that had swept us into the rocks. The rocks were too slippery to cling to and the barnacles cut my hands. Finally, we both freed ourselves from the rocky ledge and the tide and struck out for the beach, which was not far off.

Dozens of Indians were there on the beach as we staggered ashore. We were scratched and bruised but we were alive. It was sad to see the *Island Girl*, pounded by the waves, slowly drifting toward us.

The Indians gave us dry clothes and some bowls of clam soup and dried beef. We were exhausted and slept all afternoon and that night. In the morning Captain Nidever rode up to talk to us.

"If there is anything left of the *Island Girl*," I told him, "it is yours, if you want it."

The boat had washed ashore and was in splinters.

"There's good wood left in her," he said. "I can use it."

I handed him the compass, which I had wrapped in oilskin before we left the ship and wore around my neck.

He unwrapped it and took some directions. "Good as new," he said. "Never thought I'd get it back. I'll use it when I go to the Island of the Blue Dolphins."

"When?" I said.

"Soon."

"When?" I asked again.

"Maybe in three months. Maybe sooner. Maybe later."

"Can I go with you?"

"We'll see," he said, putting the compass in his jacket. "Women aren't good luck on a ship."

"I brought the *Boston Boy* good luck. They harpooned four whales while I was aboard the ship."

"*Boston Boy*?"

He looked surprised so I told him what had happened to us on the whaler. When I had finished the story he still looked surprised.

"You're lucky you didn't end up in Boston," he said.

"Can I go with you?" I asked him again.

"I'll think it over," he said.

11

Every week during the rest of the summer I went down the beach to see Captain Nidever. Just before fall I saw him at the Chumash village near Ventura. It was a pretty village that sat on the curve of a shallow headland with a white beach in front of it. The Chumash kept their canoes on this beach and it was here that I found him talking with three men.

I waited until he was finished talking and then I went and stood by his horse. After he came over and got on his horse he looked down at me and smiled.

"I'll be going out to the island one of these days," he said.

"When will it be?" I asked him.

He pushed his hat, which had a high crown and a silver band around it, far back on his head.

"Well, I can't say exactly. Depends."

He was thinking and I waited for him to get through.

"I bought two canoes from the Chumash," he said.

I did not know why he needed two but I did not ask him.

"I'm lashing the canoes together, with a little deck between. That way we can put up a bigger sail. We can go faster and bring home more pelts with two canoes lashed together with a deck between. I am using some of the wood from what is left of your boat. What I need now is a stout sail."

"I can weave a sail, Captain Nidever. I have woven many mats at the Mission."

"It'll need to be stronger than a mat and tight to hold the wind."

"I can do both. I can weave the sail from reeds and young willows." In my excitement it did not matter to me that he was going to the island to kill otter and not to find Karana. "I can weave it as strong and tight as you wish."

"How long will it take?"

"I can only work at night," I said. "In the daytime I have to work for the Mission."

Captain Nidever pushed his hat back again. "Let's see. This is August. Could you do it by September? Around the middle."

I counted the days on my fingers. I counted the

hours I would be able to work at night, since the lamps were put out at nine o'clock. I worked it all out by making marks in the sand.

"September," I said.

"Good," Captain Nidever said.

The Captain turned his big white horse around.

"The footprints you saw on the island last summer," I said. "How many did you see?"

"I didn't count them, miss. But I'd say a dozen or more. Looked as if whoever it was saw us first, ran out of the water across the sand, jumped up on a rock, and climbed a steep cliff. Scared, I guess, of white men."

"You are sure it was a girl?"

"Sure of it, as sure as you can be of anything. Not small feet, exactly, but not big either. Sort of in-between. A man wouldn't have been scared of us, I don't think. Any girl would run and hide, if she had any sense, that is."

I would have been scared, too. Neither Captain Nidever nor a friend of his named Curt were kindly looking men. They both carried guns and daggers. It would be wise to run from them and hide and not answer when they called.

I had been thinking about this for many months now. It was in my thoughts so I spoke it.

"When you go to the island," I said, "if you de-cide not to take me would you take one of the padres?"

"Why?"

"So the girl, so Karana, will see that he is not like other men. That he is dressed in different clothes and carries no weapons and has a kindly look. Then her fear will not keep her from coming with you."

"My look is not kindly?" the captain asked.

"No," I said, "with all respect to you. No."

The captain laughed.

"What size is this padre? Most of them can't lift one adobe brick without dropping it on their foot."

"He's not so big as you."

"Not many are," the captain said proudly.

"But he's half as big as you. And he does not eat much."

"When you come next time, perhaps next week, bring this padre and we'll see if he's half as big. The eating, I doubt. I've never seen one yet, big or small, who couldn't eat an ox."

"His name is Father Vicente," I said.

"I don't care about his name. Does he get seasick and can he lift an oar?"

I did not know about these things—oars and seasickness — but "He is a brave man," I said.

"We'll need that," the captain said. "Bravery is good to have."

"I will bring him here," I said. "And you can look and see for yourself."

"Bravery you can't see," said the captain. "But if he has a paunch, even a little one, don't bring him. That you can see and it means only one thing."

Captain Nidever had a paunch, but he was a big man and strong. Father Vicente did not have a paunch, even a small one, but he was not very strong.

"I will bring him," I said. "And myself, with your permission."

In answer, he tipped his hat and rode away.

12

THE NEXT WEEK, with my two friends, Rosa and Anita, I went to see Captain Nidever again.

It was a windy day but the sun was bright and hot. The tide was low and we walked along the beach until we came to the place where Captain Nidever was making his boat. It looked different since I had been there last.

"You have worked much," I said to him.

"Done the hardest part. The rest is easier," Captain Nidever said.

"I came to see how big I must make the sail," I said.

Captain Nidever had a long string with marks on it, which he used for measuring. With it he measured the size of the sail. He cut off two pieces of string from a roll he had and gave them to me.

"One," he said, "the short one, is the width at the top and the other the width at the bottom. The sail will be almost square and the height about three times as tall as you are."

Rosa and Anita wanted to stay and watch Captain Nidever work, but the tide was coming in, so we left for home.

There was a trail to the Mission, but it was long and dusty and at this season of the year rattlesnakes came out to warm themselves. This was the time they were sluggish and did not like to run away. For that reason they were more dangerous, except in late spring when they shed their skins and were blind.

I think most of the rattlesnakes in California lived in our hills because the hills were so sunny. And all kinds lived there—some were the color of the brown manzanita bush and some the color of gray granite and some had dark diamonds on their backs.

They would always run away or try to hide, unless they were blind and sluggish; but I was scared when I saw one, like everyone else, even though I always felt sorry for them. It must be terrible, I thought, to be something that everyone fears and hates and tries to kill if they can.

We girls chose to walk along the shore, which is longer, but it was still light when we got home. I started to weave the sail that night. Rosa and

Anita decided to help me, but I would rather have done the weaving alone. I really wanted to make the voyage to the island alone. Although I had never seen Karana I had a great love for her and I did not want to share it with anyone. I was very selfish when I was fourteen. I am still selfish but not so much.

Because Father Vicente had given us the afternoon to go to see Captain Nidever, we had to work extra. An hour that night in the kitchen and two hours in the morning making things that the Mission sold to Yankee traders, and again in the kitchen the next night.

It was two days, therefore, until we could work again on the reed and willow sail.

About a week later we finished it and took it to Captain Nidever. The sail would have fit perfectly except that he had decided to lessen the height, so we had to trim the edges and bind it with heavy cord.

Father Vicente went with us to talk to Captain Nidever.

"Do you think that it would help for me to go along?" Father Vicente asked Captain Nidever.

"Can you catch otter?" the captain asked.

"I am not a hunter," Father Vicente said. "But I can wield an oar. I have traveled the big river in Panama with a canoe."

"The sea and the river are different."

"They both have their problems," Father Vicente said. "Have you ever traveled a river where there are crocodiles everywhere? As far as you can see there are eyes watching you, bobbing up and down like corks, but watching?"

"That I haven't done, nor do I intend to," the captain said. "But I think we have a better chance of finding the girl if you go with us. Not so many otter, however. Do you want to go? We don't promise you anything, Father, but a rough voyage. The girl may not be on the island at all. The footprints could belong to someone else. Probably do, but we can make a try. Curt and I aren't going out there to chase around over the hills and rocks looking for a girl. We're going to catch otter. If you want to see if you can find her, it's all right with me."

"I will go. Now. Tomorrow. Whenever you wish," Father Vicente said.

I had always loved Father Vicente since I first came to the Mission, but never so much as I did now. He was a small, thin, young man, pale and not very strong. Why should he go many miles through the rough seas to an island of rocks and treacherous winds to search for a girl he had never seen? Why should he search for someone who might not even be alive or there on the island at all?

I asked him. "Father Vicente," I said, "why do

you risk your life for a girl you have never seen?"

He squirmed around in his gray robe. "There is little risk. Captain Nidever is a good sailor. He has been to the island before."

"What if he cannot find it? What if he sails past the island and falls off where the ocean ends?"

"The ocean goes on and on, so he will not fall off."

Father Vicente did not want to explain why he was risking his life. "Your aunt must be lonely living there by herself for so many years," he said.

"Yes," I said. "I would not like to live alone."

"Without God," he added.

I said no more, knowing now why he was going far out to sea among reefs and high waves and wild winds.

Captain Nidever looked closely at Father Vicente and for a long time as if he were measuring the size of a piece of timber.

"We're going to the island for otter," he said. "We require space for the pelts we bring back. You look as if you'd take up little room, about as much as three full-grown otter, so I guess we can take you." He turned to his friend, Curt, who had come with a bucket of pitch. "What do you think?"

Curt said, "He can go in my place."

I guess Curt must have been joking because Captain Nidever laughed.

"Next week," the captain said, "if the good weather holds."

"I am ready any time," Father Vicente said. "Let me know the day before you leave."

"I would like to go, too," I said to Captain Nidever. "You told me once that you would think about it."

Captain Nidever replied, "I've thought. I've given it much thought. Many times."

I could tell by his words and by the way he said them that he had made up his mind.

"You could cook for us and use an oar if need be, but we lack room. There is no place for you in such a small boat."

I said no more. I could tell that he had never thought of taking me. But still I was happy that someone was going at last. Whether I could go or not mattered only to me.

13

On Friday of the next week Captain Nidever came to the Mission and told Father Vicente to get his things ready for they would be leaving at sunrise.

"A small bottle of fresh water is about all you'll need," he said. "Maybe a strip or two of dried beef. And a heavy cloak and cowl. It won't hurt to bring a knife, too."

Everyone helped to get Father Vicente ready. Even Madre Enrica, who looked after the kitchen and the place where we all slept and did not like to work much, helped.

We found him a small olla that had a handle and would hold two gallons of water. We packed ten strips of dried venison, each strip a yard long, and wrapped each of them well. Anita and Rosa and I worked most of the night and knitted him a cowl that fitted his head tight and came down over his shoulders. We knitted it with red wool and put a tassel on top, so we could see him when he was still far off. We polished the best knife in the armory, the one that had a long, curved blade with an ivory handle. Father Vicente thanked us for our trouble, but did not take the knife with him.

Long before dawn I was awake and dressed and out on the beach. It was not long before most everyone was on the beach. The tide was low and we walked down to the Chumash village near Ventura. Father Vicente looked paler than he usually did. I guess he was thinking about getting seasick already.

Captain Nidever and Curt had dragged the boat to the water's edge and they stood waiting for us to come and help them. For some reason the Chumash did not offer to help them. I think it was because they were very religious people and did not think it right for white men to kill otter and sell the pelts to other white men. That is what was said, but I do not know.

The tide was out and the surf was coming in knee-deep, so we had no trouble pushing the boat into the water and beyond the small breakers.

Then while everyone shouted instructions to Father Vicente, Captain Nidever put up his square sail we had woven and the boat moved away to the west. It went very slow. For a long time I could see Father Vicente's cowl bobbing up and the red tassel waving in the wind.

When the boat had disappeared Gito Cruz, who was the *mayordomo* of the Santa Barbara Mission, motioned us to follow him and we went back to the bluff above the beach at Santa Barbara.

He turned around and faced the ocean and pointed. "*Mira*," he said. "Look, and you will see the boat."

We all looked where he was pointing and to our surprise there was the boat again, the square sail and the three men.

"Why can we see the boat now but when we were on the beach it had disappeared?" my friend Rosa asked.

"Very *insignificante*," said Gito Cruz, who liked to talk in Spanish and English both, often at the same time. "You see," he said, "the world is round like the orange. When we were there on the beach we could see a certain distance because the earth, being round like an orange, curves away from us as we look at it. But when we stand up here on the cliff we can see beyond the curve. Understand?"

He looked around to see that everyone knew what he was talking about and everyone nodded to let him know they understood. I nodded my head also, although I did not understand about the world being round.

"If we go higher," he said, "if we climb up in the belfry, we will be able to see them when they are even farther away than they are now. Understand?"

Yes, everyone understood. They understood him much better than I did.

I went into the Mission and to Father Vicente's favorite chapel and knelt down and prayed for him. I prayed that he would reach the island without being too seasick and that he would find Karana and, although he would have to sail uphill when he came back—if Gito was right about the world being shaped like an orange—he would bring Karana back safely.

After that they sent us back to work to make up for all the time we had lost on the boat and on Father Vicente. The girls went to the looms and the men into the fields. We all worked hard and two hours longer than usual to make up for the time we had lost.

Before dusk I climbed to the belfry, which was against the rules, and looked out to the west. I had a clear view of the sea because the Mission sat on a hill, but I saw nothing except water stretching away and away and lots of waves with white crests moving shoreward on the west wind.

That night the thought came to me, as it had before: What if the men found Karana on the island and brought her back with them to the Mission and she did not like the Mission, nor her new life, nor us? She would be used to her own ways on the island, doing what she wanted and living as she wanted to live. When she came to the Mission, she would no longer be able to do those things. She would have to live as I lived and all the Indians lived, in the way the Father Superior wanted us to.

It was a strange thought. It made me unhappy and kept me from going to sleep.

14

EVERYONE SAID we would have a good spring so
Gito Cruz decided to plant early melons. The
Mission had a small valley about half a league to
the east that was surrounded by hills of rich soil
and protected from the wind.

It was here he took us when the boat had gone
and we had eaten our breakfast. Usually only the
men went to plant melons, but we had sickness at
the Mission that year. (Since the Yankees began
to come there was much sickness that the Mission
did not have before.) But this time, because of a
sickness, which they called measles, the girls had
to help in the fields.

The soil in the valley was rich, as I have said,
and because it was sheltered it was hot, which is
good for the growing of melons, but not for working.

The *mayordomo* laid out straight lines with a string and a team of oxen pulled a plow along beside the string. This made every row straight. Gito was a clever young man about many things and he raised the best melons of any of the Missions.

Rosa and I were working together, planting the seeds stored from the year before, making small holes and dropping seeds into them. At melon planting time Mando always had fishing to do. He was now with some gringos fishing south along the coast. He liked anyone who fished, gringos or not.

We did it carefully because if the seed was not planted properly it would not sprout. Gito always went down the rows about three weeks after the planting and if he found places where the seeds had not sprouted, he got very angry and made us plant them again.

He came up now as Rosa and I were working. It is hard work, stooping over that way—up and down, up and down—in the hot sun. He was carrying an olla of cold water and he passed it to us.

When we had finished drinking, he said, "It is a hot day, *verdad*?"

"True," I answered, "it is hot."

"But the sun is good for the seeds, *verdad*?"

"True," I said.

He took a drink from the olla and wiped his

mouth with the corner of the handkerchief he wore around his neck. Gito always dressed well. Even when he was working, he wore clean shirts and handkerchiefs and boots with stitches on them.

"The sun is good for the melons," he said, "but not for those who plant them."

Neither Rosa nor I said anything.

"It is hard work for girls," he said. "It is harder work than the looms. Do you not agree?"

"Harder, yes," Rosa said.

"I do not like the idea of girls working in the field," he said.

I knew what the *mayordomo* was coming to, but I did not show that I knew.

Gito Cruz had come to the Mission two years before. He was the son of a man who was the chief of a small tribe that lived about ten leagues north of the Mission. Gito did much grumbling when he first came to the Mission, I was told, so the fathers made him a *mayordomo*. He felt this was a position more fitting to the son of a chief.

But Gito still grumbled after he became a *mayordomo*. I knew from other times that he was getting ready to grumble now.

"They work us hard here at the Mission," he said. He looked at me. His eyes were small but very bright and he had a mustache as thin as a thread, which he plucked carefully every day.

"Where do you come from?" he asked me. He had asked me this before.

"Far to the east," I said.

"If you were there would you be working hard in the hot sun?"

"We work and rest, both," I said.

"When you wish—one and then the other. We do not do that here. We are not allowed any wishes. Here we work every day, sun and rain, winter and the summer. Sometimes I stop and I ask myself, *Mayordomo*, why do you work so hard? Do you ever say this to yourself?" he asked Rosa.

"Sometimes."

The *mayordomo* went away to talk to the other people who were planting seeds. He gave them a drink from the olla, talked for a while, made jokes, and went down the other rows talking and handing out water.

Everybody looked up to Gito, not only because he was the son of a chieftain and a *mayordomo*, but because he was an Indian. Everyone felt he was a friend, and therefore an enemy of the white man, who had taken our lands, an enemy of this new world that the gringo had brought that was so hard for us to live in and understand.

We planted melon seeds until the bells rang at dusk. Then we started back to the Mission for mass and supper.

I have spoken of our *mayordomo* as Gito Cruz. Perhaps I should say that we all called him "Manos de Piedra," which he liked better than his real name, because he had fists like stones and a heart that I think was stone too.

Anyway, on the trail home, Stone Hands said to Rosa, "Are you tired, *muchacha*?"

"Yes," she said.

"This happened before you were born," he said, speaking to us all. "I was not born then either but I have heard. This was when the first Mission was built away from here in San Diego. The Indians did the building, the hard work; they got tired, tired as we are now, and one night they burned down what they had built and fled into the mountains. They went back to their homes."

We had come to the top of one of the hills that enclose the valley, from where we could see the Mission and its belfries.

"The Mission in San Diego was made of wood," Stone Hands said. "But our Mission is made of mud bricks so it will not burn. Not much of it anyway. There is little to burn. But we can go away. We can leave the Mission and go back to our homes."

Stone Hands had spoken this way before but no one ever thought he was serious about it. But he was serious now, looking at each of us to see that we were listening.

"On Sunday night. This one that comes," he said, "there is a fiesta. After the fiesta everyone goes to their rooms. The girls to their rooms, the boys to theirs. We will not undress. We will pretend to sleep, but when the bell rings for ten o'clock, each one will get up and bring his blanket."

He looked around to make sure that everyone heard.

"The doors are locked," someone said.

"Do not worry. I will take care of the locked doors," Stone Hands said. "All of you will move quietly on bare feet. We will come together in the garden. Nobody will appear except the young. The old women and the old men will stay. And when the bell strikes we will meet. I have food hidden away to last for many days. We will take the food and our blankets and go to the river. There we will walk toward the north, in the water that leaves no prints. We will walk all night and reach a cave I know of and sleep. The soldiers will not hear that we are gone until morning. There will be no prints to say which way we have gone."

We all stood, saying nothing, looking down at the Mission. Everyone thought that Stone Hands wished to make himself the chieftain of a tribe. And there were many who would follow him. But not all. A few hesitated. These he knew by name.

He spoke to them now, each one, and to all of us.

"They have come to our villages and taken us away by making us great promises," he said. "They have taken us to their Missions and made us work. If we do not feel like working they flog us. If we run away they send men to bring us back. Is this not true?"

Everyone said, "Yes, it is true," even those who from fear hesitated. "Not always, but sometimes."

"We leave our villages because of promises," said Stone Hands, "and the promises are seldom kept. If they work us from dawn until dark. If they punish us when we do something they think is wrong. When we can endure no longer and leave they send their vaqueros after us with chains and muskets." Stone Hands paused, waiting for his words to be heard deep and felt in the heart. "If this happens to us, then I ask you all, those especially who cannot make up their minds one way or the other. I ask you, what are we?"

He waited for an answer.

"Slaves," said my friend Anita.

"Slaves," others said.

"Slaves," everyone now said, even those who had not made up their minds before. It was not true that we were slaves. The fathers at the Mission wanted us to believe in their God and they made us work hard and were strict and often were impatient with us. Yet they loved us as if we were their children. Everyone sided with Stone Hands because they liked and feared him both and because many of them felt like slaves.

Stone Hands said, "Since we are slaves, what is left for us? What is the thing we can do?"

"Flee," one of the workers said and then everyone nodded his head and said, "Flee! Flee!"

He paused again and waited a long time. Then he said, speaking each word slowly, "If anyone here says a word, this I promise him." He drew a finger swiftly across his throat.

We started down the hill to the Mission as Stone Hands went on talking.

"San Diego, our brothers burned down long ago. And they burned San Juan Capistrano. This Mission of Santa Barbara was shaken down by earthquakes. It was burned by fire. The sweat of Indians has put it back together from the earth four times over. We have lost our lands to the Missions and the gringo. But our lands and forests and rivers we shall take back. Again they will be ours. And remember my warning, all of you, each of you alike. You know me, Stone Hands. You know that I do not speak words just to hear them." Again he drew a finger across his throat.

At the bottom of the hill, just as we were going through the gate into the Mission, he took my arm and pulled me aside. He waited until everyone had passed us and gone into the Mission.

"Some asked about the locked doors," he said. "There are two, as you know. The door from the boys' quarters is locked. The door from the girls' quarters is also locked."

He turned his back upon the Mission and faced me. "Wrap this in your shawl and show it to no one. I made it from the key the old lady carries around. I got it from her when she was asleep and made one like it. I have tried the key on both of the doors and it works."

He laughed. "I should become a locksmith." With these words he put the key in my hand and I slipped my shawl over it. The key was heavy and awkward. I took it at once to my bed and hid it under the blankets.

Before the bell rang for mass, I climbed into the belfry and looked off toward the west in the direction the boat had gone, thinking that something might have happened to cause them to return. But I saw nothing on the sea. The water was calm and the nearer islands of Santa Rosa and Santa Cruz stood up very clear against the sky.

Beyond them, far out where it was sometimes stormy it was also calm. But I could not see the Island of the Blue Dolphins because it was too far away, perhaps because the world was shaped like an orange, like Stone Hands said.

After mass Father Merced talked to us while we ate but many were not listening. They were thinking about what Stone Hands had said when we had come home from the fields.

15

Stone Hands had chosen Sunday night because of the fiesta, but also because of the full moon, which would make traveling easier.

It was a quiet fiesta. There were paper globes, which had colored candles in them, looped around the courtyard and three boys played guitars and one played a violin and everyone danced, even the old ones. It should have been a noisy fiesta but everyone was quiet, thinking his own thoughts.

Stone Hands danced with me first.

In the few months I had been at the Mission he had paid more attention to me than to any of the other girls. He brought me a flower sometimes, which he picked in the garden. No one else was allowed to pick flowers from the garden, except the padres. Sometimes he brought me a sweet from the kitchen, which he was not supposed to do either.

But when we were in the fields or were dancing he said very little. Usually, he asked me where I had lived before I came to the Mission. He asked me this over and over. I guess he could not think of anything else to say. Sometimes I told him different stories.

I did not want to get married. I was fourteen years old and the age when most of our girls got married, but I did not want to.

Especially, I did not want to marry Gito Cruz. I did not like the way he talked or did not talk, or the way he made his mustache into a thin line, or the name he chose for himself, or the way he strutted around. There was nothing I liked about him at all.

My friend Rosa said, "You will get used to his mustache."

"Maybe to his mustache," I said, "but not to all the other things. Marry him yourself."

"I would if he would ask me," Rosa said.

As we danced that night, Stone Hands said, "You have told me about your aunt who may come back from the island. I understand how you feel. I understand that you would not wish to go away and have her come here and find no one she knows. I understand all these things. So I do not expect you to come with us tonight. Later, after one moon, I will send you a message and tell you where we are. Then you will come to us with your aunt. I will send you a map, which will tell where we hide."

"I will think about what you have said," I replied, but I did not want a map, nor did I wish to know where they would hide.

It was nearly the end of the fiesta and we were dancing gravely together, saying little to each other.

Anita danced a bamba, which is difficult, with a tumbler of water on her head, while with her feet she picked up from the floor a handkerchief with two corners tied together.

Then Rosa danced a jarabe with Stone Hands, while singers stood in a circle and broke in with short verses. She held her skirts above her ankles to show off her feet, which were tiny, and the rest of us drummed with our heels.

One of the boys had gotten a dozen duck eggs from somewhere, emptied and then filled them with perfume water that he got from Rosa. He pelted all the girls he liked with the perfumed eggs, which made them shriek and chase him through the courtyard.

Again Stone Hands and I were dancing together, saying nothing to each other.

Then he said, "I have asked you where you came from. I have asked many times and each time you give me a different answer."

"I am a Digger Indian," I said. The Diggers were the lowliest tribe anywhere on the coast. They lived near San Diego and got their names from the gringos because they spent most of their time digging roots out of the ground.

"Someday you will tell me the truth." He smiled and his thin mustache twinkled, but he was angry. "Someday before long, before I die, perhaps."

"I will tell you now so you will not have to die waiting. My mother came from the Island of the Blue Dolphins. As you already know, she was the sister of Karana who is the girl who still lives on the island and has been there since before I was born. Our tribe when the ship brought them to Santa Barbara did not like it here and they left. You know this also."

"There are many that think the same," Stone Hands said. "At every Mission from San Diego to San Francisco, they think the same."

"I do not know where any of them went except my mother," I said as we danced slowly around and around. "My mother married an Indian from Mission Ventura and went to live at Pala which is a village south of here many leagues."

"I know Pala," Stone Hands said. "The Cupeños owned a wonderful country of streams and plumes of steam that came out of the ground and thousands of acres of grazing land and many cattle and horses. You know what happened then? A gringo came and married a young lady who was brought up by the governor's mother."

I knew this story and it always made me mad to hear it. It still makes me mad.

"Warner, the gringo, got his wife to talk to the governor's mother, who talked to the governor himself, and then within the time of two moons the land of the Cupeños, which they had owned for hundreds of years, was given to Warner. A gift of fifteen square miles of the best land in California was made to a gringo. Just as though you were passing out a plate of beans, he received fifteen thousand acres. You know what happened to the Cupeños?"

"I remember."

"They were moved away, many miles away, to a place that even the coyotes shunned."

"That was where my mother lived and where I was born and where my mother died of a disease the gringos brought," I said.

"You know what I talk about therefore."

"Yes," I said, "I know it well."

Never again would Stone Hands have to ask me

where I was born when he could not think of anything else to say. I would have told him before if all of this had not been so bitter to think about and to say.

16

When the fiesta was over and everyone went to bed I waited until the bell in the big tower struck. This was the signal I had waited for.

I slipped out of bed and found the iron key that Stone Hands had made. The other girls—there were fifty-nine of us—were out of bed now and were fixing their blankets into tight rolls.

I went to the door that led outside to the hallway and downstairs into the garden. I put the key into the keyhole. I was fearful that it would not fit, that it would go into the keyhole but not turn the lock. I worked quietly and carefully.

The door made a squeak, as it always did, but it came open. In their bare feet, clutching their blankets, the girls passed me and went silently down the stairs. Then I opened the door to the boys' room, although I did not like what they were going to do. They were ready and came out fast, but noisier than the girls. In a moment I heard them in the courtyard, just a faint sound of bare feet moving away.

I went back to bed and hid the big iron key under my blankets. In the morning I planned to take it down to the beach and throw it into the sea.

Now that our people were outside I was sure we would not fail. Stone Hands had told me that while the fiesta was going on he had put a powder in the glasses of the overseers, the two men and the two women. It was a powder that he got from plants that grew wild in the hills. Just a little of it put you to sleep for hours. You awakened with a headache but nothing else.

The five fathers had not taken any of the powder but they slept far off from the main building. Therefore they heard nothing that night.

The first word arrived at breakfast when only the old women and men came down to eat and found bare tables. The commotion was great. The old people, fearing Stone Hands, would say nothing to Father Merced, who asked the questions. He then asked me what my thoughts were.

"Do you know where they have gone?" he asked.

"I know little," I said, which was the truth.

"Why did they leave us? We treat them well."

"Because they are used to living in another way."

"They like living in squalor, in brush huts, on the beach with no roofs over their heads? Not knowing where their next meal will appear from? Eating roots and grasshoppers? Living not in the presence of God but with the devil himself?"

Father Merced was a serious man with glasses who read many books and prayed for hours at a time. He had white hair that was like wire and stuck up straight all over his head, except where his tonsure was.

"They prefer this life?" he said.

"They seem to," I replied.

He gave me a sharp look. "Why are you here? Why are you not with them, since you apparently believe as they do?"

What I would have answered, I do not know, probably not the whole truth, because just then Captain Cordova came into the room. He was the head of a garrison of would-be soldiers that lived a league away, guarded the Mission, and sponged off of our labor.

He bowed to Father Merced. "I have just heard the news. It is not more than an hour ago. I have ten men with me and we have ridden without stopping since the word came. I can tell you, sir, that we will have them all before night falls."

Captain Cordova turned to me. He was short

and stout and he wore boots that came up to his waist and a leather *cuero* that would stop any arrow. He held his silver helmet across his chest in deference to Father Merced.

"What do you know?" he said, turning to me.

"She knows nothing," Father Merced replied.

"Is she deaf?"

"No," I said. "I do not know where they are."

"Did you know of the plan? Did you hear about it yesterday? The day before? Sometime? These things do not happen in one night."

"She knows nothing of value," Father Merced answered.

Captain Cordova bowed again. "We will find their prints and follow them. You will hear from us before nightfall."

But at nightfall there was no news of Stone Hands and his band of girls and boys. Nothing except word from a sheepherder that he had seen smoke rising in a place where he had never seen smoke before. It was to the south, five leagues away in the direction of Mission Buena Ventura.

There was no one left to do the work at the Mission, and the dinner hour seemed lonely and quiet.

At mass that evening Father Merced asked us — those few of us who were left — to pray for the runaways. I prayed for them with all my heart, not that they would "see the light" as Father Merced

106

told us, but that they were safe and happy where-ever they were.

Afterward I left the chapel and went outside and down to the beach. Waves were coming in and running up the sand. I knelt down and prayed to Mukat.

In the beginning of the world, according to our tribe, there were two gods, Mukat and Tumaiyowit. The two gods quarreled about many things. Tumaiyowit wished people to die so the earth would not be crowded. Mukat did not. Tumaiyowit went down to another world. He took all his belongings with him, so people die because he died.

I prayed to Mukat for the runaways and for Karana. I had already prayed to the white man's god and now I prayed to our own. I thought that two gods would help me better than just one.

Then I decided to pray to Coyote because Mukat, in the time of creation, had become quarrelsome and people got very tired of him. They burned Mukat but Coyote saved his heart and ran north with it and wherever he went Mukat's dripping heart left quantities of gold.

But at last, before bed that night, I went to the chapel of the Virgin and prayed to Her as Father Vicente had taught me to pray.

17

In the morning Captain Cordova came to the Mission with three of his men and asked Father Merced if he could talk to me.

Captain Cordova was waiting in a small room Father Merced used sometimes for an office. His mustaches were curled and his gold buttons shone and his high leather boots glistened.

The captain was very polite. He bowed to me, which he never did to an Indian.

First he gave a short report to the father. The meaning of it was that they had not found the runaways but that his men were on their trail and success would come at any moment. Then he turned his gaze upon me. His eyes were polite also. He did not look at me as he usually looked at Indians, as if they were some sort of strange creatures that he neither had seen before nor wished to see again.

"What is your name, señorita?"

That was another thing they did not do, these officers. They never called an Indian girl señorita.

I was suspicious and began to be afraid.

"My name is Zia."

"Zia what?"

"Zia Sandoval."

"You are an Indian and you have a Spanish and Indian name. How is that, señorita?"

"Because my father's name was Sandoval and my mother called me Zia. He was a Spaniard and she was an Indian."

The answer did not seem to please him, but he went on.

"Why is it that you failed to go with the runaways?"

"My aunt is coming soon from the island."

"You wish to be here at the Mission when she appears?"

"Yes."

"If your aunt was not coming, what would you have done?"

"About what?" I asked.

"Would you have run away with the other Indians?"

I liked the fathers, some more than others. But they all had been kind to me. And Father Merced had given Father Vicente permission to go off to the island, with the chance that he would never return. And Father Vicente himself had made a voyage that few men would have the courage to make.

He had gone because, as he said, "It is hard for me to sleep and think of a girl living there on an island alone with no one to talk to. And certainly without the Lord's blessing, because she knows nothing of our Lord, if I may judge from what you have told me."

Captain Cordova repeated his question. "Would you have run away had it not been for your aunt?"

I did not want to hurt Father Merced. Or Father Vicente. Nor did I want to give Captain Cordova anything that he could use against the Indians who had gone, or against me.

"I did not go. Is that not enough?"

"No," the captain said. "It is not enough. It is not an answer to my question."

"That she is here and her aunt is coming here, should be an answer," said Father Merced.

He did not like the garrison. None of the fathers liked it. All of them wished that the garrison would move far away.

"Do you know, señorita, that the Indians stole property that belonged to the Mission—clothes, blankets, pots, food?"

"I know nothing about stealing."

"Do you know that stealing is a crime?" Captain Cordova asked me.

I was silent, not knowing what to say.

"Do you know where the Indians are hiding?" he suddenly asked.

I shook my head.

Captain Cordova walked to the door and nodded to the soldiers who were lounging outside. They came into the room and two of them took me by the arms.

Father Merced lifted himself from his chair and went and stood in the doorway, blocking their path.

"You have no right to take this girl," he said to the captain. "You have no right in this room or on this land. It belongs to the church. I order you to leave at once."

The captain made a gesture to his soldiers. Father Merced still stood in the doorway and blocked their path.

"My dear Father Merced," the captain said politely, "some of what you say is true and some is untrue. If you do not care if the Indians steal your blankets and your food, that is not my business.

This is your church and if you want them to steal everything in it and the church itself, that too is not my business. But the Indians you protect killed, as they ran away, two steers and two calves that belong to Don Blas Corrientes and six sheep that belong to Don Baltasar Moreno.

Captain Cordova put his hand on Father Merced's shoulder.

"The gentlemen do not like their cattle to be killed. And who can blame them? They came to me, therefore, and demanded that I do something. So I do something. Do you wish me not to do something? Do you wish me to mock my position as commander of the garrison? No, of course not. So I come here to talk to the one Indian who did not run away, who did not steal blankets and food, who did not kill cattle and sheep. As you suggest I will leave your church, but with me I will take the girl who is a friend of the runaways and who only stayed behind for a personal reason."

"Let the gentlemen whose cattle were killed make their complaint to the gringos," Father Merced answered.

"The gringos will do nothing," Captain Cordova replied.

It was true that the gringos would do nothing. What went on between the Spaniards and the garrison and the Mission was none of their business.

"The gringos will laugh in their sleeves at me and at you likewise," Captain Cordova said.

He put out his hand and pushed Father Merced aside. "With your permission, we will now leave," he said. "We have much to do."

He nodded to the soldiers and they took me outside and put me into a cart and drove me off to the garrison.

18

THE GARRISON was built by Indians from the Mission, using adobe bricks. It lies on the edge of a low bluff. At high tide when the sea comes in waves beat against the rocks that it sits upon.

The room where they put me was three paces one way and four paces the other way. The floor was made of mud mixed with ox blood. It was very hard and cold. In the wall that faced the sea there was a slit and a heavy door. The slit was too small for even a child to crawl through and it had three square iron bars but no glass.

A very fat woman, who moved up and down more, as she waddled along, than she moved forward had charge of the women's part of the garrison. Her name was Señora Gomez.

She closed the door behind us and told me to undress. She hung my clothes carefully on a peg fastened to the back of the door. From a reed bag she carried under her arm she drew forth a thin cotton shift and told me to put it on, which I did.

"Now take off your sandals," she said in a sweet voice, "and put them beside your bed."

My bed was a pile of straw in one corner of the room and beside it I placed my sandals.

I looked at her for a long time, until she looked at me with her little black eyes that peeped out from folds of flesh.

"Why do you take my clothes away?" I asked her, already feeling the cool breeze from the sea and the cold, hard floor.

"It is orders," she said, still speaking sweetly. "The orders come from the capitán. I do not ask him why he gives the order, I just do what he commands."

Señora Gomez left me an olla of water and five tortillas. "These will last you until tomorrow," she said, pushing herself into the doorway. Half-way through she stopped and said, "El Capitán is a wise man. What he asks, I advise you to answer truthfully. That way it is easier for you."

She pushed herself further through the door and with a final gasp reached the outside. She closed the door and barred it and went away.

I went to the window and looked out. I could see the islands and whales spouting in the long curving channel. The tide had ebbed and birds were running along the edge of the waves dipping their beaks in the sand as they fed.

The sun went down and the sea came in and beat against the rocks below the garrison, sending gusts of spray through the barred window. No one came near nor were there any sounds above the beating of the surf.

It grew cold. I tried covering myself with straw from the pallet in the corner, but every little while I would have to get up and move around the cell to keep warm. I put a bundle of straw on the floor and stood upon it and jumped up and down. Before morning came I thought I had frozen and nothing, no sun ever, would thaw me out again.

In mid-morning Señora Gomez came. She was too short to see through the window so we talked through the door.

"Did you have a good night's sleep?" she asked.

"Excellent," I said.

"Were you warm enough?"

"Yes, very warm, thank you."

"Good," she said and went away.

In an hour she was back with four tortillas. She opened the door a crack, shoved them through, closed the door, barred it, and disappeared.

The sun came into my cell in the afternoon. I

grew warm again, but I dreaded the night when I would have to jump up and down to keep from freezing.

A ship had sailed into the channel and anchored about a league offshore. The sun was in my eyes and at first I thought that it might be Captain Nidever's boat that had come in. But it was a Yankee whaler, trailing behind it two dead whales. At once the men began to cut the whales up with their knives and toss chunks into pots. Great plumes of black smoke began to rise and float across the channel and into my cell.

At dusk Señora Gomez came again and talked through the barred door.

"El Capitán has returned from Ventura," she said. "He is very tired from his long journey but he wants me to ask you if you have changed your mind."

"Changed it about what?" I asked.

"The runaways and the stolen goods and the slaughtered animals—all those things."

"I know nothing," I said.

"Shall I tell him that you know nothing?"

"Tell him what I have told you," I said, "and may you go with God."

The second night in the cell was much like the first. I moved around and made bundles of straw and jumped up and down in my cotton shift as I had before. I was cold all night and could scarcely move by the time the sun came. But somehow it was not so cold as the night before.

I said to myself, "I can do this for a long time. I can be silent until they get tired of me." I spoke bravely to myself but I did not feel so brave.

Early the next morning Señora Gomez came again to the door and asked me if I had enjoyed a good night and all the rest of the speech she had been prompted to say. I answered her the same as I had before. A little later she brought me tortillas and water.

The sun came in and warmed the cell. The whaling ship was still cooking whale fat and the smoke still drifted into my cell. I looked out but the dolphins were not playing in the channel nor the live whales spouting, and I braced myself for the night.

19

In the afternoon Señora Gomez returned and handed me my clothes and told me to put them on.

She took me to the office of Captain Cordova, which was a dozen times the size of my cell and had many windows with red shades on them and a big lamp hanging down from the ceiling. It must have held a hundred candles and they were all burning.

He was seated at a desk and behind him against the wall was a stack of muskets, lances, and swords, and something that looked like an iron glove. He seemed to be in a bad humor. This time he did not address me politely as señorita. I took this to mean that the soldiers had not found Stone Hands.

"When we were talking the other day," he said,

"I asked if there was any way you could help us. I told you and the good father who is growing a little simple in the head that what happens at the Mission is his business. Likewise, what crimes take place on land that does not belong to the Mission, land which belongs to men like Señor Corrientes and Señor Moreno, is my business. Do you remember?"

"Yes, I remember."

"Do you also remember that I asked you if you knew where Stone Hands was hiding?"

"Yes."

"And you said nothing to my question. You only shook your head. Now I ask you again, do you know where the Indians hide?"

"I do not know," I said, speaking the truth.

"They would go and not tell you where they were going?"

"Stone Hands said he would send me a message," I answered, truthfully again.

"And that message you have not received."

"No, sir."

"Do you expect to receive a message?"

"It is possible."

"Anything is possible. Will you receive a message from the Indians? Yes or no."

"It is possible," I repeated. "It is that and nothing more."

Capitán Cordova pulled at his nose, which was long and thin and for some reason a little crooked or his face was a little crooked, one or the other.

"I have talked to the matron at the Mission. Señora, señora . . ."

"Señora Gallegos."

"Yes, to her. And she says that both the door to the men's quarters and to the women's quarters were locked the night the Indians fled. She remembers locking the doors especially that night because she had heard some of the Indians grumbling and making threats.

Capitán Cordova rose and went to the window and closed a curtain that allowed the sun to shine in his eyes. He started to walk around the room. He passed the stack of muskets and the lances and the swords, picked up the iron glove, tried it on. Then he dropped it on his desk and sat down and lighted a cigar that smelled worse than the smoke from the whales.

"A *viejo*, and old man in the shop, tells me that he found some of his iron missing the morning after the Indians left. It was the kind of iron that he makes keys out of. Do you suppose that sometime that night Stone Hands in some manner got hold of Señora Gallegos' key and went to this shop and made himself a key? A key that was exactly like the other key, a key that would fit the doors perfectly. Do you think he would do a thing like that?"

"He could," I said. "He is clever."

"So being clever, he made a key," Capitán Cordova went on, "to fit the locks. Since the doors do not open from the men's quarters he must have given this key to one of the girls."

The Capitán carefully tapped the ash of his cigar into a tray and glanced up at me as I stood in front of his desk. I felt embarrassed and afraid.

"This key that he made, did he by chance give it to you?"

I was silent.

"He gave the key to you so that you could open both the doors."

"There were more than fifty girls and women in the room that night," I said. "Why should he give it to me?"

"Because you are his close friend," Cordova replied. "You are the one he knew the best and could trust."

"He knew many girls and he could trust all of them," I said.

The capitán cleared his throat and puffed on his cigar.

"When does your aunt come?"

"Soon," I said. "Soon, I hope."

"Do you want to be in the cell when she comes?"

"No, sir."

I felt like saying that Señor Corrientes had ten thousand cattle and would not miss one or two. And that Señor Moreno owned more sheep than he could count. But I kept this to myself.

"Well, we surely hope not, since we are noted here in Santa Barbara for our hospitality. Perhaps she will not come soon, maybe tomorrow or the next day or next week. Perhaps meanwhile you will receive a message from Stone Hands. Suppose all this. And suppose also that when this message comes you give it to me, Captain Cordova. Then we can all catch this clever fellow who calls himself Stone Hands and give him a little punishment. Then we can all be hospitable together and welcome your aunt to Santa Barbara.

We can have fiesta with music."

He stood up and shouted for Señora Gomez.

"In the meantime," he said, "perhaps we can learn who it was that used the key that Stone Hands made. The doors into the boys' quarters did not open themselves. They are not magical doors."

Señora Gomez came waddling in and stood sleepily in the corner.

Captain Cordova picked up the iron glove from the desk and put it on his hand. "It does not fit so well," he said, "but it is not supposed to fit well. I have another glove just like it. They have much weight. They are very inconvenient."

The glove had a screw on one side and he began to turn it. He turned the screw until it was tight. He lifted his hand above his head. I could see that it was very heavy. Then he let his hand with the iron glove drop on his desk. The sound was loud. Señora Gomez opened her eyes.

"I never use this unless I am forced to. I am a kind man, of a good disposition, and very patient."

Captain Cordova had no real authority over me. Years ago, when Mexico owned the land, he could put an iron glove on me that squeezed my hand until I screamed, as he had done to the hands of many, so I had heard. He was trying to scare me and he could try only because Father Vicente was away. If Father Vicente had been home, he would not have threatened me. For some reason he did not fear Father Merced.

He was enjoying himself, I could see. And while he had no authority for all of his threats, there was nothing I could do. I was helpless and fearful, as he meant me to be.

He unscrewed the glove and put it on his desk. Then he nodded to Señora Gomez, who came and took me to my cell.

That night after supper I heard a scratching at

the bars of my cell, then a voice. It was Mando, who had come back from fishing.

"I have food for you," he whispered.

Through the bars he passed me a strip of meat that he had saved from his supper.

"Tomorrow, Zia, I will bring you more."

"*Cuidado*, señor," I said. "There are many ears that listen. This is all they have to do."

"I will take care," he said. "But if they catch me they catch a mountain lion. They will not like the lion they catch."

The meat was tough but it tasted good after the water and stale tortillas.

20

THREE DAYS went by. A north wind brought a storm that lasted for two days.

I wondered where Captain Nidever and his boat were. I wondered if they were safely at the island or whether the storm had caught them somewhere. It was very cold and Capitán Cordova sent orders that my clothes were to be given back to me and an extra blanket as well.

The Yankee whaler had finished cooking blubber and the air was clear once more. Now that the whaling ship had gone, the dolphins came back. I could see them through the barred slit playing in the sea beyond the breakers. And the whales came back and sent up their feathery spouts.

On the sixth day Capitán Cordova sent for me and I went into his office. The first thing I saw was the iron glove on his desk and its mate beside it. He seemed in good spirits, puffing away on a cigar, with his broad-brimmed hat with the gold braid tilted back on his forehead and his stitched boots on the desk.

"I have good news," he said. "At least I think the news is good. One can never tell about news. It is like cream. It can turn sour between the cow and the kitchen."

I waited for the news, knowing that it could not be good for everyone, that for someone it would be bad.

"Don Blas Corrientes reports," the captain said, "that Stone Hands and his band are camped at the head of the creek that runs through his ranch. They are camped in a box canyon and can get out only by the trail they used going in. It is a simple matter to have Don Blas's vaqueros and my soldiers flush them out and march them back to the Mission."

He paused to examine the screw on one of the iron hands that lay on his desk. I wondered what this had to do with me. He must know by now that I had received no message and if I had it would not concern him. He had Stone Hands and all my friends cornered in a box canyon from which they could not escape. What did he want of me? Why did he frighten me with an iron glove? Why did he keep me freezing in a cell that I scarcely could turn around in, with straw to sleep on and a barred slit to look out of?

"How long have you been here at the Mission?" he asked me.

"For many moons."

"Where did you come from?"

"From Pala."

"I know the place. It is where the Cupeños lived after they left Warner Springs. Why did you come from Pala?"

"Because of my aunt. I heard that she was living alone on the island."

"And you thought by coming to Santa Barbara you might find someone who would go out and search for her."

"Yes, sir."

I still had no idea what he wanted from me.

"You have been here for a long time." He paused and looked at the end of his cigar, which had gone out. "In that time you have had a chance to observe the various fathers?"

"Yes, sir."

"You have talked to Father Merced and have talked to other Indians who have talked to him. You have worked at the looms and the garden under his instructions."

"Yes."

"Tell me," the capitán said as if suddenly we were old friends talking together, "do the Indians, the girls and boys, like this man, Father Merced?"

"They like him," I said.

"You speak without much conviction . . ."

"Then I repeat, the boys and girls respect Father Merced."

"Respect?" Capitán Cordova lighted his dead cigar. It had an odor that was worse than before.

"Why if the boys and girls respect him so much," Capitán Cordova said, "why then do they run away from his Mission?"

"I do not know," I said.

"Do the others feel happy in Father Merced's care?"

"There are some who do and there are others . . ."

"Who would like to run away and not come back."

Capitán Cordova hated Father Merced. Everyone at the Mission knew that. They knew also that Father Merced hated the capitán. Father Merced had complained about the capitán and his drunken soldiers, and Captain Cordova had complained about Father Merced. It was not a new quarrel, from what I had heard. It was a quarrel that had gone on now for most of a hundred years—this rivalry between the garrison and the Missions.

"You yourself have spoken to me here in this room as if you would also have run away except for your aunt who is coming or who is not coming. One or the other. Why do you want to run away?"

"I would not run away," I said. "I would leave if that was the way I felt."

"But if you left, if you did not run away but just left, why would you do so?"

"Because I did not like it here at the Mission," I said truthfully. "That would be the reason."

"Because of the way you are treated. Because you are made to toil long hours. Because you are told what to do at all times. Because Father Merced is a man with strange ideas about Indians and thinks that they should be busy all the minutes of the day."

I began to have suspicions that I had not had before. Was it this hatred between Father Merced and Capitán Cordova that had caused the trouble for me? Was this why I was locked up in a cell with no clothes and little food?

"All I can say to you, Señor Capitán, is that I am here. I am not with Stone Hands and his band."

Capitán Cordova rose from his desk. He went to the door and opened it to let in some fresh air—even he could not stand the stench from the cigar—tossed the cigar over the bluff into the sea, closed the door, and came back and sat down.

"The governor gives out bad cigars," he said, speaking, I guess, to himself. "Perhaps, because he does not smoke and knows no better."

He opened a drawer of his desk and drew forth an object that I did not recognize at once.

"You have spoken several times of your aunt," he said in his polite, dovelike voice. "You have told me that you had nothing to do with the runaways."

He paused and held up the object he had just taken from his desk. He turned it this way and that and then dropped it on the desk.

"Señora Gavilan," he said, "who is, as you know, your overseer, made a search of the quarters at my request. In your bed . . ." He paused and glanced up at me. "In your bed, underneath the blankets, she found this key. It is the key that fits the lock in the men's door and that of the women. It is this that opened the doors and permitted Stone Hands and the others to flee."

"I have seen this before," I said. "I used it to open the doors." They had searched my bed before I had had a chance to throw it into the sea, as I had planned to do.

Capitán Cordova put the key in his desk. He then shouted for Señora Gomez, who came wandering in and sleepily took me to my cell. She closed the door and barred it tight.

21

Señora Gomez brought my clothes back and a blanket, as Captain Cordova had told her to do, so I slept warm that night.

In mid-morning when Captain Nidever sailed into the harbor I was standing in my cotton shift.

I saw the boat far out beyond where the Yankee whaler had been anchored—when they were only a spot on the bright sea. There was a fresh wind behind them and they were moving fast. First I could see that there were four people in the boat. I saw Father Vicente and his red tassel flying. Then I could see that one of the four was a woman.

I stood there at the window holding on to the iron bars. For the first time in many days I felt warm. I forgot that I was in a cell, in a cotton shift, with my long hair uncombed.

The boat came up to the edge of the surf, where the swells were getting ready to break. The sun sparkled on the water and in the glare I could make out the figure of Karana. She was crouched on the little platform Captain Nidever had made and I had woven the sail for.

The surf was not heavy that morning, but Captain Nidever waited for the break between waves that comes every few minutes. He waited too long and missed a time of calm. At that moment Karana rose and leaped from the boat and began to swim toward shore. A dog leaped in after her.

At first I thought that she had jumped to lighten the boat so it could be handled easier in the surf. But I am sure that it was not for that reason. She had jumped out of excitement.

The place she must have dreamed about many times was near at last. She swam strong, her brown arms reaching out. Then she was past the surf and was walking toward the shore, her arms outstretched as if to embrace everything that she saw. The dog followed along behind her.

She came out of the water and stood on the hard sand, her grass dress clinging to her. She seemed to be trying to look everywhere at once, at the low bluffs, the long curving beach, the green hills that were now red with poppies, the church. Its bells were ringing and she held herself still to listen.

The boat was coming in now between two

breakers. She turned back to meet it, but it passed her in a last rush and slid onto the beach.

I could barely get my hand between the bars, but I waved to her. She did not see me. I called her name so loudly that Señora Gomez came waddling out of her room and told me to cease.

There was a path that led up the bluff a short way from where I was locked. Father Vicente, walking unsteadily as if he were still at sea, saw my hand thrust through the bars. He stopped as I called out his name. He said nothing to Karana but then they both came toward me. They came to the barred slit in the wall and halted.

"What has happened to you?" he said, looking in at me as if he did not believe his eyes.

I told him in as few words as I could. At once he left and went into Capitán Cordova's office. I could hear them begin to shout at each other even before the door closed.

Karana stood looking at me through the iron bars. She must have known me at once because I looked like her sister. She touched my hand and held it for a moment. It was hard and rough and her nails were broken. I pressed my face against the bars and she did the same and our lips met there between them.

I spoke to her in Spanish, but she shook her head to let me know that she did not understand. Then I spoke, using the few words I remembered from a song my mother had once sung to me. Those words she might understand, but they meant nothing to her. She spoke back and her words were strange to my ears. We stood helplessly, our hands touching, gazing at each other. She looked like my own mother, as I remembered her, only younger.

I heard Captain Cordova shouting, using a different voice than he had used with me. Between times I could hear the voice of Father Vicente. This talking seemed to last for a long time. Then Father Vicente came out with Señora Gomez and she opened my cell and dropped my clothes on the floor in the doorway.

I put them on and the three of us walked up the trail to the Mission, with the dog at our heels. He was big and shaggy and looked like a wolf. When I tried to pet him he backed away from my hand.

There were many wild flowers beside the trail, but mostly a blue flower like a spike with blooms. Karana picked two of them and gave one to Father Vicente and one to me.

22

THEY GAVE Karana a bed beside mine in the big room where all the girls slept. She was not used to sleeping in a bed and sometime that night she got up and lay down on the floor. Her dog, which she called Rontu-Aru, lay down beside her.

Señora Gallegos did not like this sleeping on the floor. Nor did she like the dog sleeping in the room. This most of all.

"Dogs should sleep outside where they belong," she said. "They have fleas and soon we will all have fleas."

She talked to Father Vicente about the dog Rontu-Aru. But he must have differed with her, for the next night Karana again slept on the floor and the dog slept beside her.

Then Señora Gallegos went to talk to Father

Merced, who was Father Vicente's superior. Since the day of the fight with Capitán Cordova he had been ill in bed and we all prayed for him to get well. He disagreed with Father Vicente and the Señora told Karana that she could sleep on the hard floor, but that the dog would have to sleep outside in the courtyard with the other dogs.

The Señora told Karana what the Father had said, but Karana did not understand and I was of little help. She did the same thing she had done the nights before and when Señora Gallegos tried to move Rontu-Aru he growled at her and bared his teeth. Then the Señora called the *mayordomo* and he got some boys and all together they managed to tie the dog up and take him outside.

Karana said nothing while this was going on, but when they took Rontu-Aru she picked up her blanket and followed them. That night she slept in the courtyard and all the nights for a long time, her dog at her side.

Karana and I had a difficult time talking to each other. At first what simple things we said were said with gestures and sounds that had no meaning except to us.

All of the five fathers at the Mission were skilled at Indian dialects. They were people from many tribes at the Mission. And yet none of them could understand the language she spoke. I no more than any, although I was a member of the

137

same tribe that Karana belonged to. As a child when my mother died, I knew a few words of our dialect, but when I lived at Pala with the Cupeños and at the Mission with the Spanish fathers I forgot the few words I had known.

What happened was, we lived without words, with only the touch of hands and tones of voice and a glance. We tried giving names to things.

I would pick up a shell on the beach and give it a name. In the beginning Karana tried to repeat what I had said, but after a while she gave this up.

She was amazed at the many shells we had on our beach—I felt that we had many more than she had seen on the Island of the Blue Dolphins. But she was very satisfied to hold them in her hands. The big ones, the conches, Karana would peer inside and put them to her ear. She might make a sound but it meant nothing to me, as I watched her, except surprise or delight.

She kept the shells we found, but it was the wild horses she loved.

They would come down from the mountains at dawn and sometimes at dusk, horses and their colts, wild as the day they were born, and race along the sand and through the waves, making noises that she seemed to understand. She never grew tired of watching them. Nor did Rontu-Aru. The one word she learned from me—of less than a dozen words—was the word for horse.

And yet when Father Vicente offered to put her on one of the Mission's geldings Karana backed away and shook her head. I got on the horse and walked it around to show her how easy it was, but she still shook her head.

The melon patch over the hill was another place of delight. The vines were a vivid green and had begun to send out their delicate little feelers. We went there every day.

I tried to explain how big the melons grew, pointing to my head and trying to make her see that they would also be round like my head. She understood all of this but when I tried to describe how a melon looked inside I had little success. If it was evening or early morning and the sky was pink I would point to it and try to make her understand that a melon looked like that inside.

We gave her the first melon that ripened. It was a big melon and she ate it all. She liked them more than any food we had. She would eat a whole one for supper and sometimes two.

Karana also liked to work at the looms. She had never seen one before, but in a week's time she wove as fast as any of us. The first thing she made was a cloak for me with the design of a dolphin across the back. She was proud of the cloak, so before I wore it out I put it on every day, even when the weather was hot.

I did everything I could to make her happy.

Still, she did not like the food very much and sometimes, after the first melons had gone, she would go to the beach after our noon meal and dig the big clams and scoop out a pit and roast them in a fire of dry kelp.

And though she liked the horses and the shells and the melons and the looms, she seemed to enjoy just walking along the beach with her dog the most of all.

I wanted to know about the Island of the Blue Dolphins and how she had lived there and what she had thought, but this I never learned.

23

Father Merced suddenly grew very sick. When he died there was much mourning because he had lived at the Mission for thirty-one years and knew everyone for leagues around.

In his place those in Mexico City who ruled such things put Father Vicente in charge of the Mission. But only for a short time, only until they could send someone else. Father Vicente, they said, was too young to be the head of a Mission as big as Santa Barbara.

While Father Vicente looked after the Mission and before Father Torres came to take his place two things happened.

The first thing that happened was that a bracelet of mine that Señora Gomez had taken was returned to me.

The next thing Father Vicente did was to make

a shelter for Karana and her dog. He understood that she was not used to being with many people who snored and uttered strange noises at night. So he made a good place for her in the courtyard with woven mats to cover the hard stones.

In the morning, before any of the rest of us were up, before the first bell rang, she folded her blanket and put it away and was down on the beach, to pick up shells or to look for clams, to watch the wild horses, or just to romp up and down the wet sand.

Everyone liked her, but they thought she was somewhat crazy. They had never heard of anyone who rose before the first bell and went out picking flowers or just ran up and down the beach. Only Father Vicente understood and let her do what she wished. He gave orders that she was to work only when she wanted to.

The next thing of the many things that happened during the few weeks when Father Vicente was our Superior was very important.

Stone Hands and his band were still in the box canyon on the ranch of Don Blas Corrientes. Five of his band had deserted Stone Hands and had gone to Don Blas and given themselves up. They said that Stone Hands acted like he was the chief of a tribe and ordered them around as though they were his slaves. Also they were hungry.

The five boys came back to the Mission and told Father Vicente what they had told Don Blas and said that Stone Hands would never return to the Mission.

One of them, whose name I do not remember, said, "He has muskets and powder, many swords and lances. He has twenty of Don Blas's horses. He says he is going to attack the garrison and steal all their weapons. Then he is going to attack the Mission and take its silver and money. Anyone who gets in his way, he will kill. That is what he says and we believe him."

"How many boys and men does he have?" Father Vicente asked.

"More than eighty."

"And twenty horses. Ridable?"

"Yes."

The boys went to Capitán Cordova and told him the same story. What they said I do not know. What I do know is that the capitán did not like the idea of riding into a box canyon with the fifteen men at his command. He sent for Don Blas and they both came to talk to Father Vicente.

"I have thirty vaqueros," Don Blas said. "They have lances and riatas. They are a tough bunch of men."

"And I have fifteen, equally tough," the capitán said, "that makes almost the same number that Stone Hands has."

"You are equal in numbers," Father Vicente said. "That is important."

"But they are boys and I command men," the capitán said.

"If it is the box canyon I know," said Father Vicente, "the one at the head of the Montoya stream, they will see you coming long before you arrive."

"It is that place," Don Blas said.

"Then many men will die," Father Vicente said.

The three men were talking in the courtyard and everyone could hear them. Don Blas and the capitán strode back and forth. Father Vicente stood off to one side out of their paths. He was still wearing the tassel cap I had made for him.

"You are right," the capitán was saying, "we will lose men, but we will put an end to the thieves and their thievery."

"If you put an end to them," Father Vicente said, "you will put an end to the Mission. We will have no one left but a few old men and women."

"Better to end the Mission than allow it to harbor a nest of thieves and cutthroats," said Don Blas.

Father Vicente started to walk up and down. Then suddenly he halted. His red tassel was hanging over one eye. "I will go and talk to them myself," he said.

"To what purpose?" the capitán asked.

"So they can flee again and kill my cattle," Don Blas replied.

"I have decided to go," Father Vicente said and left the two men striding back and forth.

"You will get yourself killed," the capitán shouted after him.

"In a good cause," said Father Vicente.

"In a cause without merit," Captain Cordova shouted. "Remember that you only make our responsibilities more dangerous."

"You have no responsibilities with these boys and girls," Father Vicente stopped to reply.

"Except to bring them to justice," said Capitán Cordova. "And it will not be done with words."

"We will use words instead of bullets," Father Vicente said. "If words do nothing then you can use your bullets and your swords."

"We have a good supply of both," said Capitán Cordova.

24

THREE DAYS after Capitán Cordova and Don Blas left the Mission Father Vicente set off for the Corrientes ranch to talk to the runaways.

He took me with him because he knew that Stone Hands liked me. I did not like to leave Karana in a place that still was strange to her, so she came along and also Mando, because the fishing was poor.

We went on foot, as was the padre's custom. He offered Karana a horse, but she refused. I rode a fast gelding because I did not like to walk that far and because I thought that we might need a horse. As things turned out, we did. To be truthful, we could have used two or three on our long journey to the Corrientes ranch.

Captain Cordova did not go, to his great disappointment.

"You ride there with your soldiers and your

saber rattling," Father Vicente said, "and they will flee when you are still five miles away."

"I will go alone," said the capitán.

"But your saber will still rattle."

"I will leave the saber at home."

"Your helmet will shine."

"I will leave that at home, too."

"And your horse with the silver stirrups and saddle and breast shield?"

"That I will not leave."

"Leave yourself at the ranch," Father Vicente said. "We may need you and your soldiers."

"I will settle them for good," said the capitán.

"That is what I fear," said Father Vicente.

The trail to Box Canyon through the Corrientes ranch was long and winding. There were three very tall pine trees growing on the hill behind the closed canyon and I pointed them out to Karana. She seemed to understand that we were going in that direction.

The main trail, which mostly followed the coastline, ran in a roundabout way. From time to time Karana and her dog would disappear down some side trail and we would wonder if she had gotten lost. But she always showed up ahead of us. She moved twice as fast as we did at a trot that we could not keep up with. She must have had many hills to climb on the Island of the Blue Dolphins.

We followed the stream into the canyon to a shelf of rocks where the stream began from a large spring surrounded by ferns.

We had bent down to drink when Rontu-Aru growled and we looked up to see Stone Hands standing on the rock above us.

He could see in a glance that there were only three of us and a dog, and that we were unarmed. He made a circle around the rock and came down to where we knelt.

He bowed to Father Vicente and favored me with a nod. "You have come a long way for what?" he said.

"To talk to you and your people and to see if you wish to return to the Mission," Father Vicente replied.

"To work hard?" Stone Hands answered.

"Father Merced is gone and we no longer work as we did," the padre said.

"I will not miss him," said Stone Hands.

"Do you miss the church?" Father Vicente asked him.

A dozen or more young men had gathered on the rock above the spring and were watching us. Rontu-Aru was watching them.

"You ask if I miss the church," Stone Hands said. "Yes, I miss it. The hard work especially."

One of the boys standing on the rock asked, "How do the melons grow?"

"Come and see for yourself," the padre said. "We have planted more. You should be there to eat them."

"We will have a good crop," I said, "better than the first, better than last year and the year before and the year before that, they say."

"We will come later," Ricardo Aguilar replied.

"In the middle of the night," Stone Hands said. "When no one is looking."

"Come in the daytime," said Father Vicente, "when everyone is looking. You are welcome."

Stone Hands said, "You are sure Father Merced is in the ground?"

"I helped to put him there," Mando said.

"What of Señor Corrientes and Señor Moreno? And the hombre who owns the stringy chickens?" Stone Hands asked.

"I will repay them," the padre said. "They can come and choose from our herd and our flock what you have taken."

"They have good beef," someone on the rock said. "It was sweet and tender. You did not need a knife to cut it or teeth to chew it. It was good beef."

"But the chickens were tough," Ricardo said. "Like eating a ball of string."

"You have poor teeth," Mando said, "and not many of them."

Rontu-Aru was walking around in back of us, his hair bristling. There was something he did not like. It could have been the tone of the voices of those standing stiffly, with much arrogance, on the rock above the spring. Or it might have been that he was not used to many people moving around and talking so much.

One of the boys tossed a rock in the pond when I stooped to drink again.

"The water is not endless," the boy who had tossed the rock said. "There is less now than before."

"Enough, loco," said Stone Hands to the boy. "Have you heard of courtesy?"

I glanced around. The water was low. Bushes that should have been heavy with berries were stripped bare. I saw the bones of two cows and a horse. The faces of the boys were thin. The bark of a sycamore tree was stripped bare. And when Rosa and Anita came and stood on the rock, I could see that they were thin too. A young woman was peering at me from behind a scrub oak tree. She had a baby in her arms and I could see its ribs, thin as chicken bones.

The tribe was suffering from lack of food and water. They were even eating the bark from trees. I did not blame the boy who tossed the rock into the pool to protest my drinking. Nor Stone Hands who wanted us to think that they had ample to eat and drink. They were starving. That was why he had never sent the message he had promised me.

25

Father Vicente also knew that the band was starving. I know this because he was very careful not to mention it. He understood Stone Hands's pride, that he and his people would rather starve in the barren box canyon than beg for help.

"You gain nothing by staying here longer," he said. "We have settled matters with Corrientes and Moreno and Capitán Cordova. All you need do is to follow us back to the Mission."

"To work?" said Stone Hands.

"Yes, but now there is a new Mission law. You will be paid for the work you do."

"How much?"

"Not much, because we are poor. But you will be paid what we can afford. You will have a roof and food to eat." But Father Vicente was quick to add, "You do well enough here I can see."

It was the only lie I had known him to tell.

"Yet," he went on, "you make no money. You sleep on the ground. You do not know when Corrientes and his vaqueros will attack should you choose to stay here on his land. Nor Moreno and his vaqueros."

It was plain to me that Stone Hands had weighed the prospects, one against the other, and had made up his mind to follow Father Vicente. It was decided when an unfortunate thing took place.

The boy who had thrown the rock into the pool while I was drinking now tossed a pebble that struck Karana on the chest. She clutched herself and stepped back. She was more surprised than angry. But Rontu-Aru in three long leaps had the boy by the arm.

Karana's dog was the largest dog I had ever seen. And his teeth were not the teeth of an ordinary dog. They were long and curved and very white. Father Vicente had told me once that Rontu-Aru was a wolf dog, a dog related to the wolves of the north country, from where my people had come long years ago.

In three leaps, as I have said, across the pool, knocking a girl down, he had the boy by the arm and had twisted him to the ground.

"Rontu," Karana shouted. "Rontu-Aru."

Her warning shout was in time. I think the dog would next have had the boy by the throat.

Rontu came back, again leaping the pond, and sat down by his mistress. She gave him a pat on the head and something to eat, a bit of abalone, which she took out of the bag she always carried.

Stone Hands laughed. "You do not heed me," he said to the boy who now was clutching his arm. "Maybe you will heed the dog, huh, Señor Constantino. Next time he may take your arm off. Then you will have a hard time hugging your girl who is a little large to hug with one arm."

Constantino started up the hill to where a small fire was burning and a thin rabbit was turning on a spit. He was angry.

"This Constantino knows more than anybody," Stone Hands said to Father Vicente. "More than God, I think."

Night was coming on. As it was, we would have to go the last league in the dark.

"We leave now," the father said. "We are here to ask you to come home with us. If you do not like the Mission this time, then go. I will not follow you again."

He wore a long robe. He now kilted it up around his knees, which were bony but strong. He could go all day and not tire from walking. He wore his tassled hat.

Stone Hands glanced around—at the peeled bark of the sycamore tree, at the dwindling pool of water, at the small fire on the hill and the skinny rabbit that was roasting. He glanced at the girl with the baby whose bones looked like sticks. At his back and on two sides were granite cliffs. He must have seen it all, in one hopeless glance.

For a while he watched Constantino walking slowly up the hill to where the rabbit was cooking. Now and again Constantino would stop to whack at a bush with his sharp machete.

Stone Hands called an Indian call. His group came down the hill and those at the spring gathered around him.

"We will go," he said quietly to Father Vicente and started off down the stream. "But we will not pass the ranch of Señor Corrientes."

As he spoke the loud sound of metal striking metal came from the hill where the fire was burning. Constantino had struck the pot with his knife, scattering the food and the burning wood.

Everyone stopped and looked back. Five boys had stayed with Constantino and were trying to put out the fire. But very quickly it spread. It caught the dry grass and the pine needles and in an instant began to lick at the three trees nearby.

There was a hot wind blowing from the east—the kind we call a *Santana*—and it began to fan the flames. The three pine trees became three flaming torches.

"*Vámanos!*" Father Vicente shouted.

The wind was blowing down the canyon toward the Corrientes trail, along the trail that followed the stream we had come by.

Karana said nothing but beckoned to us. One after another, keeping in line and close together, we followed her and her dog.

Great flames leaped up from the three trees. They became one flame. The wind caught it and flung it into the sky and toward the coast like a banner.

Karana was moving fast at a trot, Rontu-Aru at her heels, and we also broke into a trot. Father Vicente took the baby and Stone Hands put his arms around a girl with a bandage on her leg and helped her along.

There was a lagoon that ran along the coast and cut inland in such a way that the fire could not spread to the Mission nor to the Corrientes ranch. But the land between was aflame.

The sound of the fire was louder than the surf. We went fast, for our lives, following Karana, who must have thought of ways of leaving the canyon when we had come in the morning. She must have been in fires before.

Mando said, "We could have gone along the

lagoon to the shore." He was disappointed that now he had lost the chance to tell everyone that he had saved us from the fire. "That way we would have reached the sea. Fire does not burn the sea."

I pointed at the waves that the wind sent crashing against the rocks along the shore. "We would have drowned," I said. "Which would you prefer?"

Mando pulled at his ear. He did not like Karana very much because he could not understand what she said. He thought everyone should speak the language he spoke. Unless they did, he thought there was something wrong with their heads and he looked down on them. There were many at the Mission who thought the same. And when Karana learned a few words of Spanish, he and others would smile because she spoke the words in a way that sounded different to them.

He was now impatient. "Stone Hands and his people," he said, "follow the surf."

"Because he would rather risk his life with the sea than with Señor Corrientes," I replied. "And I do not blame him."

"I can do what Stone Hands does," Mando said.

"But you have no reason to prove it."

"I want him to know that I also can defy the sea. I may save someone, even him."

"You had best save yourself."

"He taunts me because I did not catch the big fish."

"That was not your fault."

"Also that I wrecked the boat."

"No one is to blame for the boat."

"Stone Hands thinks so."

"What he thinks is of no importance."

But before I could stop him, Mando was running off toward the shore where great waves were crashing and Stone Hands and his people were trying to make their way along the shore.

26

W<small>E COULD SEE</small> the flames for a long time. They even shone far out on the sea. But we had crossed the lagoon that ran inland near the Mission. Some lay in the grass and rested and some slept. We did not reach the Mission before daylight.

Before noon that day Don Felipe and Señor Moreno came to the Mission to protest the fire. They came with Capitán Cordova and called for Father Vicente. The four men talked for a long time in the courtyard. Then the three men left.

I was working at my loom so I heard nothing of what was said. There was much shouting and striding up and down, but when I saw Father Vicente later he said that he had convinced them all that we did not start the fire and if they wanted to find the one who did for them to go out and search.

Things were better now that Father Vicente was in charge of the Mission and we had new laws. We did not work all day and what we made on the looms we were given permission to sell to the Yankee ships that came into the harbor to trade. Part of the money we could keep and part went to the Mission. This was a new way. In the old days we were not allowed to keep money we made.

The second crop of melons swelled and grew ripe. Karana liked them so much that whenever she had a chance she would steal away and eat melons. She ate more than I have ever seen two people eat. She even ate the small black seeds. She even taught Rontu-Aru to eat them. He must have been the only dog in the world to eat melons.

When the Yankee trading ships came Father Vicente let us go out to them in our canoes and sell the things we had made and were allowed to keep. The rest of the things we made he sold himself, since the Yankees were sharp traders.

Neither Karana nor I had ever been on a trading ship because Father Merced had forbidden it before.

It was like a store on land, only it was on a ship, with rows of shelves filled with hats and beads and dresses and shoes—with everything you could find in a store on the land. Karana bought a hat that was pretty and had a ribbon around the brim and a collar for Rontu-Aru that had a silver buckle. We always liked these days.

We liked all the days now that Father Vicente was our superior, but then suddenly everything changed. In the time of one day a new world descended upon us out of a clear sky.

Sailing into the harbor came the *Buenaventura* and on it was a man with white hair and a big round face and a body so thin he must never have eaten at all. His name was Father Malatesta and he had come from Mexico City to take charge of the Mission, to take the place of Father Vicente.

The next day the ship sailed north to Monterey and on it was Father Vicente. We stood on the beach and waved him farewell and some of us cried to see him go.

Everything changed then. The new father was older than Father Merced, or seemed older. He wore glasses and looked at things over them and not through them.

He called us all together in the big chapel and told us where he had come from, and that he had heard about the trouble we had had in the past, and what a fine Mission he would make of it.

But now we worked harder and had no time to ourselves—only an hour before we went to bed. We were not allowed to keep anything of what we made.

"The church is very poor," said the new father. "We must work hard and make it a great Mission again. Greater than it ever has been."

He changed many rules and gave out a list of what we could do and not do. No one liked the ways the Mission was run now. Stone Hands began to grumble again.

But the worst change was for Karana. Father Malatesta ordered her to sleep in the *dormitorio* and because of fleas Rontu-Aru had to stay in the courtyard. Karana tied him there by his new collar. The first night no one could sleep for his howling, not even the new father.

He told the woman who was in charge of the girls' room that Karana would have to move her dog and she told Karana. I was not there when they met so I do not know how she told her. All I know is that night the dog was not tied up in the courtyard and Karana was not in her bed next to mine.

27

We all thought that she would come when the bells rang for morning mass but she did not appear, nor afterward for breakfast, nor to the room where we wove mats.

At noon I took my time to eat and went in search of her. Mando and I sometimes had gone about a league from the Mission along the sand to San Felipe lagoon and the point that ran out in the sea. When the tide was high the surf beat against the point, but at ebb tide you could walk over the rocks and around it.

On the north side of the point were two tall pinnacles and between them, hidden from view, was a cave. It was the same cave that Mando and I knew. At high tide spray beat against it, but other times the sun shone in and it was like a twilight world.

The cave curved and went far back, perhaps twenty long strides from the mouth. The roof was jagged and in places you had to crawl to get through. Then suddenly this long corridor opened and you were in a large room with long things hanging down from the ceiling, like the lights in the chapel, only they were in the shape of cones and clear as air.

The tide was high, but it was here in this big room that I found Karana. She was sitting on a rock that was as flat as a table. The tide came in and out around her. She patted her dog and spoke to him in her island dialect.

I was in the cave for a while before I saw that there were others in the cave besides the three of us.

When she lived at the Mission, Karana brought home wounded animals and birds with broken wings. I was not surprised, therefore, that she brought them here. There was a pelican with a broken leg, which she had bound up with sticks and tied together with reeds. There was an otter watching us from a pool of water near the rock we sat on. Also a gull with a wounded wing. In the twilight of the cave I saw other eyes watching me, though I could not see who or what they belonged to.

On the rock was a small fire. Karana was roasting mussels and clams, moving them around in the coals. Rontu-Aru sat with his head on his paws beside her. He had not barked when I came into the room. She must have taught him when to bark and when to keep silent. But he sat there very quietly, his yellow eyes watching everything I did.

I greeted her with a sound we had made up ourselves and it was much like any sound of greeting.

She stirred the fire and sat back and put her hand firmly on my arm. She kept it there for a long time.

From her touch I knew why she was there and why she would never go back to the Mission while Father Malatesta was there. She would never sleep in the room among many people, without her big gray dog.

She offered me some of the clams that had popped open and smelled good, but I had to leave to get back in time for work.

That evening I returned after mass. I had a hard time reaching the cave in the dark, especially since I carried with me one of the last melons from the garden.

Karana had built a large fire and was eating on the flat rock. We ate the melon. At least she did, and we sat with the firelight flickering over the walls and the cones that hung down from the ceiling and looked like crystals.

I had taught her the word for dolphins and when she used it she meant the island where she had lived before.

She pointed to the wall in front of us. It was flat and in it were the bones of something that looked like a wing, the wing of a giant bird that must have been twenty strides in length. The whole wing was there fastened like stone flat against the wall, a great hovering wing without feathers, of an animal that must have flown a long time ago when Mukat was alive and Coyote roamed the land and Zando was our god.

Karana pointed to the skeleton wing and made a gesture toward the west and said the word "dolphin." I knew that she meant that she had seen such a wing on the island where she had lived and I wondered if she wanted to return there.

Then she made an outline in the air, saying that the skeleton she had seen before had a head and beak that was much wider than she could reach. And pointing to her own eyes, she made a circle that let me know that the bones of the bird she had found on the island had eyes as large as the rock we sat upon.

We watched the giant bird with the firelight casting shadows on it. And the skeleton came alive as I watched and as the shadows changed and became feathers, each feather heavier than a strong man could lift, and I saw an eye larger than the table. It was the color of amber. When you looked at it, the eye moved away, but when you were not looking you knew it was watching you.

I quit looking at the skeleton of the giant bird. I quit thinking that it must have eaten large animals, even people, when it was alive and flew around the islands. We sat in silence for an hour or more, all the things we wanted to say to each other locked within us.

The next noon when I came again Karana was sitting outside in the sun. She looked pale and made a motion that meant she felt sick.

"Where?" I asked her, pointing at all the places where people get sick, which are many. It took me a long time.

She pointed to her stomach and made the motion of eating. Then she pointed to her head.

There was a good witch woman at the Mission and an old man who knew many cures but I could not get Karana to move from her cave.

That night when I came with the last melon from the patch and opened it on the rock, Karana would not touch it. I knew then that she was sick.

I went back to the Mission and talked to the old medicine man. He could barely walk, but in the morning, with great difficulty, I got him to the cave. We found Karana sitting on the flat rock beside a small fire. Rontu-Aru lay at her side.

The medicine man asked her questions. Karana said nothing and I reminded him that she did not understand the dialect we spoke, nor Spanish words either. He shook his head and took a pouch from the folds of his tunic and laid out some things on the flat stone—an eagle feather, a black shell I had never seen before, the long tooth of a bear, the skeleton of a fish—many things. Then he mumbled a Spanish prayer to Mukat and to Coyote and to Zando.

It was a long prayer and I could see that Karana was not listening to him. The sound of the surf and the cries of gulls fishing came from far off. I think this is what she heard.

The medicine man then took forth a flute and began to play a tune that was so shrill it was hard for me to hear. But Rontu-Aru heard it, for he cocked his ears and turned his head from side to side, as dogs do when they hear strange noises. Something else heard it too.

While the old man played he kept looking at a place above my head. So fixed was his gaze that after a while I turned to see what he might be gazing at. Near the bones of the giant bird, at a place where its mouth could have been, was a jagged hole. And in the hole was a snake's head. It had wide jaws and large eyes the color of emeralds and a long forked tongue that slowly flicked back and forth. It must have been the snake I had heard about.

Serpiente, Karana said. It was one of the few Spanish words she had learned.

It was likely one of the wounded that she had found somewhere and brought to the cave. She spoke the word without fear. If anything, she spoke with pity, pity for a creature that was fated to live its life hated and reviled by everyone.

At last the old man stopped playing. "Zando has heard my prayer," he said. "He promises to use his powers. All will be well, he says. He will speak to Mukat and to Coyote when he returns from his journey."

We walked back to the Mission and I went to the chapel and prayed to the Virgin, but while I was praying I kept thinking of the snake with the emerald eyes that came and listened when the old man played on his flute.

The next day Karana was better and she had a big driftwood fire going on the flat rock. Around it were nests of kelp. In the nests were swallows that she had picked up on the beach. Although it was spring, a cold wind had come up and killed all the insects that the swallows fed on. As I walked down the beach I had seen the swallows darting here and there along the cliff searching for food and others lying dead among the rocks.

Karana had no way of feeding the starved birds she had gathered up, but she kept them warm until they died. The cold wind left and a warm wind came and the swallows around the Mission and along the cliffs ate once more and built nests everywhere.

28

On a fine spring day Stone Hands gathered up a band of young men and girls who did not like Father Malatesta and his new ways and went off to the north. Mando went with them. He said he would leave Stone Hands soon and go to the town of Monterey on the sea.

"I may find the captain of the *Boston Boy* in Monterey and he will give me back my work. If not, there are many Yankee ships in Monterey and I will choose something that suits my talents, which people say are many."

"When you come home from your voyages, Mando, you will have many more talents. Good fortune and may God go with you."

"Coyote and Mukat will go too," he said, striding off to conquer the world.

Karana fell ill again that night and the next

morning I asked the woman who oversaw our work and each day taught us Spanish words if I could go and talk to Father Malatesta.

"My aunt is ill," I said.

"Where?" asked the señora.

"On the beach."

"Tell her to come to the Mission and she will receive treatment. We are busy here, we do not have time for illness."

I then went to Father Malatesta's office and waited there while the bells tolled three different times, counting the hours. At last a handsome young padre who had come with Malatesta from Mexico appeared and asked me what I wanted of him.

"My aunt, whose name is Karana, is ill."

The young padre apologized to me for his lack of furniture. "It has not yet arrived from Mexico," he said. "Make yourself comfortable on the sill. Why is your aunt not treated for her illness?"

"Because she is not at the Mission."

"Where is she?"

I said that she was on the beach but not where.

"Why is she on the beach?" he asked me.

"Because Father Malatesta ordered her to sleep in the *dormitorio*."

"That is where people sleep."

I told him that she had come from an island far off the coast where she had lived for a long time.

"She is not used to our ways," I said.

The young priest got up and looked out of the door. "She must get used to them. Otherwise why do we have a Mission? So everyone can do what he wishes? So dogs can run everywhere?"

"She will get used to the Mission but not now. Now she is ill."

"We can do nothing for her if she remains on the beach."

"She will not come here," I said.

He shrugged his shoulders and sat down and began to go through a sheaf of papers.

"She cannot sleep in the *dormitorio*," I said.

"Where did she sleep before we came?"

"In the courtyard with her dog."

"We cannot have people sleeping wherever they wish. Nor dogs running here and there."

He put the papers in a drawer and leaned back and put his hands behind his head and glanced up at the ceiling.

"Is your aunt feeble in the mind?"

"No," I said quickly. "But she is not used to our ways. It will take many moons for her to get used to them. I have been here for a long time and still I am not used to them."

"You have trouble, too? It must be in the family, this trouble."

"I came here but not against my will," I said. "I was happy living where I did live, in the moun-

tains. Someday I may be happy here doing what I
am told to do each hour of the day. When Father
Vicente was here I liked him and because of him
I liked the Mission. I liked God, too, and the Virgin."

This was the wrong thing for me to have said. It
made the young priest angry. His face flushed.
He got to his feet and as he stood at the door he
said, "I will see what can be done about your
aunt, who cannot sleep in a fine clean room and
without her dog. I will give it serious thought. I
may have a chance to speak to Father Malatesta
about it. He is a wise man in these matters, but
now he is very busy."

I left and went down to the cave. Karana was
lying on the flat rock and the fire was out. I
lighted another fire and sat beside her and held
her hand.

Early the next morning I went to the cave. The
sun was bright on the sea and the tide was out.

Karana was sitting at the mouth of the cave,
leaning against one of the stone pillars. She held
out her hand to me. It was small and cold.

Since the first time, the time I had seen her
through the iron bars of my cell, she had worn a
necklace. It was a pretty necklace of black stones.
They were all round and shining and there was a
spot of fire deep inside each one.

She took off the necklace and put it around my

neck. She sat back against the stone and watched the morning unfold. Pelicans were flying low over the surf and farther out young whales were sending up their airy plumes of spray.

We sat there, saying nothing, until the tide came in and the first bell rang in the belfry. Then I got up and kissed her good-bye.

"I will come back at noon," I said. "Not with a melon, though. They are gone. But with something you will like."

Usually Karana looked up at me and smiled. Then I saw that her head had turned to one side. She was looking far off across the sea. After a while I saw that she was no longer breathing.

Some thought that Karana died because she caught cold sleeping out in the weather. But she was used to caves and beaches and all kinds of weather. Others said she died of some sickness she had caught from the white traders. But these things were not true.

I think she died for a different reason. She liked the people at the Mission, although she was shut away from them because she did not speak the language they did. She liked to watch the birds feeding along the beach and the gulls crying and the spouting of the whales and the dolphins playing in the channel. She liked to watch the wild horses galloping through the surf. And the red melons with their black seeds and the dancing of the fiestas.

She liked these things but still she missed the island where she was born and had lived for most of her life. She missed it deep within herself, in a place she had no words to reach. She missed it like I missed my home in the mountains.

The next evening after mass we buried her in a place near the Mission. All the birds were flying home and the candles shivered in the cold sea wind. That night I took my blanket and slept nearby with her gray dog beside me.

At first there were many of her animals for me to take care of. But one by one they got well enough to fend for themselves. All but the snake with the emerald eyes. The last time I was in the cave he was still there in the wall by the skeleton of the great winged bird.

29

I<small>T WAS</small> still dark when I left the Mission. I took a bag with me filled with bread I had saved, a clay pot to cook in, and a blanket I had made for such a time, if it ever came. I could not handle Rontu-Aru by words so I put a riata around his neck.

We left quietly and by the front gate, where anyone could see us if they were awake. I was closing the big gate behind us when I heard a voice. It was Father Malatesta's. He was coming from the chapel and he held a book in his hand.

"You are up early," he said.

"Yes, I have a long way to go. The sun will be hot at midday."

"Where is this place you go, young lady?"

"Far away, Father, in the mountains. Ten days to the south and three days to the east."

"The place you came from?"

"Yes, long ago."

"Who gave you this permission?"

"No one, Father, I came a long while ago and now I return."

"You do not like us?"

"I like you but this is not my home."

"You do not like our food and our shelter? You do not want us to teach you skills and the grandeur of our language? You do not find God to your liking? You would rather pray to snakes and coyotes and the sun than to our Virgin Mary?"

"I am thankful for all that you have given me," I said.

"But it is not enough—all these things?"

"It is enough, Father Malatesta, and I thank you and Father Merced and Father Vicente. But God is in the mountains too. Now I go back to my home."

I closed the gate. Then a curious thing happened. Father Malatesta came to the gate, slowly, with the steps of an old man, and handed me the book he carried.

He said, *Vaya con Dios*. And I returned his farewell, wishing him to go with God, also.

I went down to the beach. The tide was out and the sand was wet. There was a glow behind the mountains, far to the east, but the sea was dark.

I walked until the sun came up and then I sat down and ate a piece of tortilla. I tied the riata around my waist for the gray dog still did not want to go with me.

I could see the black stumps where the fire had started in Box Canyon. Between them and the lagoon, for a distance of a league, the fire had burned everything. It looked like a blanket of black snow. But along the marges of the San Felipe lagoon grass was already beginning to grow.

It was not until I had walked for the length of seven suns that I let Rontu-Aru off his leash. It came about this way.

It was just before dusk and I was still walking along the beach, since it was the easiest path to the south. A man came out of a brush hut and started down the beach toward me. He said nothing, but walked along in back of me for a while.

I stopped and loosened the riata. The gray dog turned and walked toward the man, baring his teeth.

"Rontu-Aru," I called, remembering Karana's command.

The man turned away. The dog backed off, growling, and came to my side. After that I never put the riata on him again. I had no fear after that for him or for myself.

The way home to Pala in the high mountains to the south I knew. It was faster to go by land, because the shore went in and out. It is twice as far along the sea.

I did not hurry. I played stick with Rontu-Aru. I would find a piece of driftwood and throw it out in the waves and he would plunge in the water and bring it back. I pried mussels from the rocks, made a fire, and boiled them in my clay pot. I also dug clams. Some of them were bigger than my hand. I gave Rontu-Aru the tough parts, because his teeth were a lot stronger than mine and I made a stew of them with some acorn flour an old woman gave me.

It was a long way home, over a hundred leagues, but it was a happy journey. I had time to think of many things, during those first days of summer, and the last days of my girlhood.

There was a wide stream that came out of the mountains and flowed slowly back and forth between oak trees and sycamores and the red manzanita. It had a sandy bottom with patches of blue stones. The stream was near to my home. When I came to it I began to run. My dog ran at my side.